Born
SINNER

BOOK
0.5

CORRUPT GODS DUET

USA Today BESTSELLING AUTHOR
CORA KENBORN
INTERNATIONAL BESTSELLING AUTHOR
CATHERINE WILTCHER

Born Sinner
Copyright © 2021
by Cora Kenborn and Catherine Wiltcher

Cover design by Maria at Steamy Designs
Editing by Gillian Leonard
Proofreading by KC Fernandez and Ronda Lloyd
Formatting by Midnight Designs

"Every saint has a past and every sinner has a future."

—Oscar Wilde

My sins will be her penance…

I came to this college for one reason—*her.*
A cartel princess.
Mexican royalty.
Sworn enemy of the Colombian ranks I'm destined to climb.

I'm meant to hate her.
Destroy her name and sacrifice her innocence.
But Lola Carrera isn't the delicate flower her family thinks she is.
And I just took a match to her ivory tower.

Obsession is a loaded gun…
And tonight, she's waging war with my patience.

*Born Sinner is a standalone prequel to the Corrupt Gods Duet.

PLAYLIST

In no particular order…

Bad Girl - Avril Lavigne, Marilyn Manson
Bad Boys Like Me - Hell Boulevard
I Get Off - Halestorm
Bite Your Kiss - DIAMANTE
Dirty Little Thing - Adelitas Way
Hit Me Like a Man - The Pretty Reckless
Headspin - Butcher Babies
Diamond In The Rough - The Nearly Deeds

CHAPTER
One

SAM

Obsession is a loaded gun.

The bullets started firing the moment she stepped into my party uninvited in a backless dress and heels, wearing confidence as a color and her smile as a taunt. Now, she's piling into my Arabescato marble kitchen with her girlfriends and tossing interested glances my way.

She wouldn't be this reckless if she knew who I was.

Danger has a scent, Lola Carrera, and I'm fucking wearing it.

She tries biting her lower lip and flashing those baby blues at me, like every other chick in this place. When I don't react, her smile slips, and she turns back to her friends.

Not me.

I never turn away.

For the next thirty minutes or so, I watch the rise and fall of her cigarette as shitty conversation and bad music sucks everything else around us into a whirlpool of mediocrity. I see it all—even from halfway across the crowded room of a five-thousand-square-foot apartment that a trust fund puked up for some over-privileged offspring.

Namely me.

When she sparks up her fifth Marlboro—*chain-smoking tonight, Lola?*—I track the silver trails to her mouth again, noting the shallow inhale and the subtle wrinkling of her nose. She doesn't like the taste, but she's playing a role at this college that demands an addiction. *Too bad it's not the one her daddy sells.*

I note every head tilt, every flick of her hair, every curve of those luscious ruby lips. I do it all with the same sick fascination I've been fighting since the day she arrived on New Jersey's Rutgers campus at the start of the semester. We've never spoken, we've never even touched, but you could say she fucks my mind on the regular.

I hate her.

I want her.

Taking another swig of beer, I focus on what she really is to throw cold water on my obsession. She's a two-faced innocent—a name I've been taught to hate all my life. A name I had every intention of exposing when she and her cunt brother, Santi Carrera, least expected it.

That was before I laid eyes on her.

"You want in on this, Sam?"

Lucas hands me a lit stub, and I accept it without thanks—declaring my dangerous mood to the world with a couple of savage tokes. Unlike Lola, I prefer to savor the burn of weed and nicotine instead of exhaling it fast like it's a bad word on a priest's tongue. I like the way it fills up every space in my lungs, because nothing else in my life will ever feel this whole.

"María! Hey, María!"

A loud voice rises above the music, making Dua Lipa marginally more bearable. We turn to find some prick named Troy Davis pushing through the party with a clear destination.

Her.

Yes, her. Because "Lola" isn't the name she trades under on American soil. "Lola" gets left behind the minute she crosses the border to disguise the fact that her daddy heads up one of the biggest drug cartels in Mexico. I'm betting her clique of virgin suicides would be kissing a new ass pretty damn fast if they knew she was a bona fide cartel princess.

But I know...

Let's just say I have connections, no matter how hard my senator stepfather tries to keep them from me.

"Aww, she's so *fuckable*." Lucas follows my gaze as my palm curls into a fist. "Word on the street is that her V-card is as good as her credit rating. You should totally hit it, bro. You've crushed more cherries on this campus than the juice bar."

"Are you still here?" I flick the dying stub at his chest, and he jumps back with a yelp, brushing imaginary ash from his designer shirt.

"What the *hell*?"

"Relax," I murmur lazily. "I'm sure Daddy will buy you a new one if you ask him nicely."

Lucas's stepfather is a big-shot politician in Washington too. We both have bank accounts that reflect the need for us to stay the fuck out of the headlines.

Troy's all up in Lola's face now. His arm keeps slipping around her waist.

I've never wanted to spill blood so badly.

"Who ordered the jock entrées?" I hear Lucas say in disgust. "Want me to call security?"

"Security" is a light word for the two heavies my stepfather insists on me keeping around. Senator Sanders's history of making enemies has created a claustrophobic existence for all his kids.

"Not yet." I crack open another bottle of Bud—my fourth. My head is starting to buzz, but it's doing *jack shit* for the thing I want it to dull the most.

"Suit yourself." He shrugs and starts chatting up some passing blonde. He knows there's no point in arguing with me. Besides, Rutgers's star quarterback is about to get his ass handed to him by yours truly, especially since I just watched him slip a tab of something extra special into Lola's Bacardi and Coke.

I catch the smirks on his teammates' mouths. I taste the acidity in Troy's intentions. Lola Carrera's precious V-card is about to be spanked and shredded all over my apartment, and she's not going to know a thing about it.

Unless...

The slow burn in my chest ignites, bursting into a dull red flame.

Obsession is a loaded gun, and tonight my patience is dead and bleeding.

No one, I repeat *no one*, gets to suck or fuck that body, other than me.

CHAPTER
Two

LOLA

Trust no one. Suspect everyone.
The last words my father said to me before I left Mexico ring in one ear as Troy Davis's drunken shouts fill the other.

"María! Hey, María!"

Pinching the cigarette between my fingers, I lift it to my lips and inhale while pretending not to notice. The truth is, I'm still getting used to that name.

María.

I hate it, but it was a small price to pay in order to trade my sheltered existence for the American dream. *American freedom.*

My grip tightens, denting the filter. I don't feel so free right now. In fact, I feel more suffocated standing inside this lavish New Jersey apartment than I did locked inside my gilded border cage.

Blend in, Lola...

I've barely thought the words when a rush of heat ignites, licking along the skin on my bare shoulders. Glancing out of the corner of my eye, I track his movement.

Or lack thereof...

Sam Colton hasn't moved in fifteen minutes. I know; I've counted every one of them. He's still leaned against the far wall, his heel lazily braced against it as if daring it to crumble.

Daring it to deny his weight.

His hard, muscular, sinfully defined weight.

Exhaling a cloud of smoke, I glance down at my feet, ignoring the high-pitched chatter spreading like an infectious disease all around me. *This was a bad idea.*

I'm about to spout off a lame excuse and get the hell out of here when a figure appears behind me, and hot breath fans across my neck. "Damn, baby, look at you..."

Note to self: American men can't take a hint.

Sighing, I take another long drag off my cigarette. *Dios mío, these things are disgusting.*

Already planning my exit strategy, I glance over my shoulder to find Troy pressed way too close, his hooded gaze slowly sliding down my body.

Additional note to self: American men are also transparent as fuck.

Once he finally manages to look me in the eyes, he flashes a wide smile. I'll give him full marks for effort, but it's anything but sincere. Those perfect white teeth might as well end in two sharp points.

"That dress should come with a warning sign," he notes, trailing the back of his knuckles all the way down my arm to my wrist.

Lifting my chin, I blow a steady line of smoke right in his face. "It does: 'off-limits.'"

Those blond eyebrows raise toward a perfectly styled blond hairline. It's obvious he's confused as to why I'm not already on my knees sucking his dick—just like every other female at this party wants to.

The seething hatred coming from all four corners of the room is hot enough to spark a fire. There are at least half a dozen girls here willing to sell their souls to be me right now.

All because Troy Davis is a trophy dick.

Even with my short amount of time on campus, I know every facet of the *unwritten rule*: if given the opportunity to spread your legs for the star quarterback, you don't ask questions. You do it, then wear it as a badge of honor.

Maybe if I were any other girl.

I down half my rum and Coke, my gaze wandering over Troy's shoulder. Like a magnet, it settles back on that wall… and on *him*.

Sam Colton.

My brain spins a hundred different reasons as to why I should look away, but I don't. Instead, I memorize every strand of that messy dark hair and every inch of those tribal tattoos licking up his neck.

And if he were any other boy…

One I haven't been warned to stay away from with no explanation as to why…

I'm ripped away from Sam's cold stare as Troy winds his arm around my waist and pulls me against his chest. "Come on, don't be like that, María. I'm just being friendly."

Pinche sangrón. I clench my jaw, caging the insult behind my lips.

You're not royalty here, Lola.

You're a wide-eyed college student.

Just like the herd of half-drunk coeds standing in front of me. The ones winking at Troy's arm and giving me a wave of "thumbs up" signs.

Oblivious girls bleeding their naivety all over Sam Colton's apartment.

Sam...

Flicking a gaze over Troy's shoulder, I catch him passing a dangerous gaze at us before curling his lip. My hand trembles as I lift the red plastic cup again. I wish he'd stop staring at me like that.

Like I'm a stain on his precious marble flooring.

"Right," I mutter.

Chuckling, Troy brushes his lips against my ear. "Trust me," he whispers, tracing his index finger across the back of my hand.

Trust no one.

No one is your friend, cielito. They're only an enemy in waiting.

Suspect everyone.

Everyone is a snake. Some are just better at shedding their skin.

I swallow my father's warnings, liquid sloshing over the rim of my red cup as I jerk my hand away. *If I don't occupy my mouth, my true colors will fall out...* Troy's eyes follow every movement as I lift my drink, downing what's left. Just as the corners of his mouth tip up, I step forward.

Rules were meant to be broken—especially unwritten ones.

"Trust is earned, Troy." Flashing him a syrupy smile, I drop my half-smoked cigarette into his beer, accompanied by a chorus of horrified gasps.

My name is molded around multiple variations of "whore," but I'm already halfway across the room by the time they catch up to me.

Perfect, Lola. That was the exact opposite of "blending in…"

I'm supposed to swoon and bat my eyes. Instead, I placed a tiara on my head and unloaded a gun into the wall.

Safely immersed within the bowels of a makeshift dance floor, I sneak a look back at my friends. Their mouths are still gaping in shock. I let out a rough sigh while pretending to dance to the irritating base rattling the windows.

There will be a slew of questions waiting for me tomorrow. Apologies will have to be made. Bombs will need to be diffused. Diversions will have to be crafted…

But tonight, instinct is pumping too hard through my veins to ignore.

You don't grow up as the daughter of a kingpin without learning how to carve through bullshit to extract the truth. Troy Davis's truth is what makes him so dangerous. He's a viper hiding behind Polo shirts and boat shoes.

Luckily for me, I can read asshole frat boys.

As my gait slows, I glance to my right where a pair of midnight eyes are still watching me.

But not him.

I'd have better luck reading in the dark than reading Sam Colton.

I should be home.

I should be on the couch in my favorite pajamas watching Netflix, forgetting I ever agreed to come tonight.

But I'm not.

Twenty minutes after ditching everyone, I'm still leaning up against a wall at this party. At Sam's piece of shit—gritting my teeth, I look around at the marble and crystal *everything* and sigh—at his infuriatingly beautiful apartment.

"Why the hell am I still here?" I grumble out loud—except what falls from my mouth sounds nothing like what was in my head. Instead, it sounds like one long word dipped in caramel.

My stomach sloshes around at the thought.

"This is why Santi told you not to drink, Yola." I blink. "Loya." I blink again, the weight on my neck causing my chin to fall forward. "Yoya…"

What the hell kind of rum is Sam serving?

My head flops back, slamming against the wall with a hard thud. "Ow…" *That's going to hurt tomorrow.* I try to lift my hand to rub it, but the weight from my neck is now wrapped around my wrist. So I stand there, head back, knees bent, and arms heavy, swaying to a dancing orange light.

Up.

Down.

Left.

Right.

I blink again, the clouds in my eyes thinning enough for me to realize the light isn't dancing—it's moving.

And it's not just a light.

It's a fucking joint.

Squeezing my eyes shut, I count to five before opening them, only to collide with a familiar tattooed hand lifting the joint to a familiar mouth as familiar lips wrap around the end.

Sam.

As if I spoke his name out loud, he turns toward me. This time, he doesn't look right through me. He levels that icy glare like an earthquake, and I shiver under its weight. He's less than twenty feet away, but he might as well have me pressed against the wall with both hands wrapped around my neck.

My pulse races…

I can't breathe…

It's only when he pins me with that lethal stare again that I see it…

Darkness.

He's not just a rich bad boy with a chip on his shoulder—he's a jagged reef lying beneath a calm sea. And this place isn't just an apartment—it's a diamond-encrusted snake pit.

The realization is too much. The weight is too heavy. Both tangle in a knotted haze, dragging me down the wall. Just before I hit the floor, an arm hooks around my waist, pulling me to my feet. My brain barely stops spinning when a pair of lips press against my ear.

"What do you say we go someplace more private?"

I nod slowly, the words sounding thick and muddled in my head. Then I'm floating. Fingers dig into my arm, guiding me up, up, up…

So far up, I wonder if we'll ever reach the top.

I wonder what would happen if he let me go. I wonder

how long it would take to hit the water. To sink beneath the surface and onto the reef... To stain clear blue water murky red...

My head lolls back. "Sam?"

A dark laugh rumbles beside me. "I'll be whoever you want me to be, baby."

"I don't feel so good, Sam."

"Don't worry..." he assures me. "Now that I've got that attitude dialed down, I'll make you feel better. *Trust me*."

CHAPTER
Three

SAM

I sense the brunette while she's still circling, but I'm not quick enough to dodge the swoop.

"Hey," she chirps, crinkling her eyes at me. "Cool party, huh? Love the apartment. Your folks must be loaded."

Yeah, with piles of dirty money.

"Thanks," I say dryly, looking right through her. The roofie Troy slipped Lola must be out-of-this-world phenomenal. She's already swaying in her heels.

"Wanna give me a guided tour?"

Oh, Jesus... She's cute, but there's only one woman here who makes my dick hard.

"Maybe later," I lie.

Troy has Lola by the arm and he's guiding her toward the open glass staircase. By the time they reach the second floor, she's all over the place—her long, dark hair messing up her face as her head flops sideways onto his shoulder; her dress riding up to expose more tan skin.

"Okay, well, make sure you come find me…" Brunette trails off as I push past her like the devil himself is hot on the heels of my Amiri check sneakers. Meanwhile, Lola's friends are waving her off with catcalls from below, looking as dickmatized by Troy Davis as she appears to be.

"Have fun, María!"

"Don't do anything I wouldn't do!"

Choke on those grins, you stupid bitches. She's a fucking Carrera. Don't they know she's smarter than that?

She shouldn't even be at my party. Her brother would never allow it, not if he knew my real last name was Sanders instead of Colton. I took my mother's maiden name the day I enrolled at Rutgers. Lola and I are both here under false pretenses to protect us from the war that's raging up and down the East Coast.

There's an invisible line drawn down this campus. It's the same one that divides New Jersey and New York, her family from mine, truth and lies… *Me from her.* We stay the fuck away from each other, or people die.

Santi Carrera is happy to enforce the rules for his baby sister, but he's not around right now and I get the feeling she had a little something to do with that. She's fighting for her freedom, just as much as I am, and that makes her fucking irresistible.

I move toward the stairs, fire and ice surging through my veins.

Protect her.

Reject her.

This contradiction is giving me a headache.

"Nice party, Colton."

Troy's crew try to block my access. All it takes is a single look from me and they're like sliding doors at the mall.

Pussies.

"It'd be even better without the dickhead parade showing up."

"Aw, you serious?" They clutch at their chests, all offended, like I just gang-banged their moms.

Fucking idiots.

"Get the hell out of my apartment," I say coldly.

"Or what?" says one cocky asshole.

"Or you won't be playing football for the rest of the season." I meet each of their shocked expressions in turn. "It's hard to find your own dick, let alone run ten steps, with two fractured ankles."

They wince.

"You're a sick man, Colton."

Tell me something I don't know.

I take the stairs three at a time and head straight for my bedroom. I know the mind games that provocative pricks like Troy Davis like to play. There's no love lost between us, and he'll come twice as hard knowing it's my bed he's defiling as well.

If he's touched her already...

Behind the door, it's a scene from every college chick's worst nightmare. Lola is passed out on the bed, her black minidress and heels already discarded on the floor. Troy's standing over her with his jeans around his ankles.

He looks up and smirks. "Come to join the party, Colton?"

"Consent's a tough word to purchase from the unconscious, frat boy." I glance at Lola's breasts in that black lingerie and feel my own traitorous dick stir. "You sure she's selling?"

"What's it to you? Pissed I'm buying first?"

"Wrong answer, asshole. Your libido lost its way, and the rest of you is about to pay." Reaching into my back pocket, I pull out the silver pocket knife the senator bought me for my eighth birthday. I learned to demand respect long before I learned to drive. I learned it on an island a long way away from a man who I have every intention of working for one day, no matter what my stepfather has to say about it. *You can't keep the bad away from the bad. We're like magnets around one another.*

Troy glances down at my hand, and the blood drains from his face. He yanks up his jeans and backs away from me like I'm the goddamn antichrist.

"What the *hell*, Colton? If you want the bitch so bad, you can have her."

"Did you touch her?" I tap the exposed blade against my lower lip as I saunter deeper into the room.

I find my answer in Troy's silence.

I press the blade into my lip until I can feel something hot and wet running down my chin. "Did you taste her?"

Troy looks like he's about to shit himself. "Just a kiss, man. I swear. I-I didn't know she was your girl."

Damn right, she is. "Didn't your mom ever teach you it's wrong to steal?"

"My mom's best friend is a vodka bottle. She didn't teach me *nothing*!"

"Poor little rich boys of the world unite." I swipe a hand

across my jaw and it comes away red. "Get on your knees."

A tic jumps to life in his cheek. "Wh-what?"

My foot connects with his thigh, and a dark satisfaction fills my soul as he goes crashing to the floor. Crouching over him, I take his jaw between my fingers as he cringes away. "You fucked up, Troy Davis." With my other hand, I press the blade against the nervous glide of his throat. "You just violated my property, and that shit has consequences... Lift up your shirt."

He freezes. "No way."

"I said, lift up your *fucking* shirt."

A trembling hand shoots out and wrenches up his white Moncler Polo. "What the hell, Colton?" he says again weakly. "You a queer now?"

"No, Troy. I'm your end game." Changing my mind at the last second, I drop the knife from his throat and drive it down deep into the web of muscles above his kneecap, twisting as I go, severing a couple of tendons and all his hopes and dreams. Never mind a season on the bench; I've just gone and annihilated a promising football career at the age of twenty.

I feel nothing about it, though. No guilt. No regret.

Sweet. Fuck. All.

I told you I was ready for the big league, senator.

Troy screams, and I slam my hand across his mouth. "Inhale the pain," I order, bringing my face close to his. "Inhale it until you feel like your lungs are gonna explode, because that's only a fraction of what 'María' would have felt tomorrow morning if I hadn't shown up in time." Flashing him a grin, I pull the knife out, eliciting another muffled scream. "If I were you, Troy Davis, I'd get to a hospital in the next twenty minutes. You've had yourself a bad accident... Maybe you shouldn't drink so much next time. You feeling me?"

He nods, eyes glassy with pain. Compliant as a child.

Maybe he knows the truth about me. Maybe he's heard about the senator's reputation.

Removing my hand, I wipe his spit down the front of his polo shirt.

"Go... Get out of here."

"I-I can't move." He starts crying, snot trailing down his face like a well-fucked pussy.

Are they tears of relief or pain? Maybe it's the realization he'll never score a touchdown again. Either way, I doubt he'll be slipping a roofie into another chick's drink this side of never.

"Then you crawl, asshole. I'll count to ten, and then I'm introducing my knife to your other knee."

"Shit! Fuck! Okay!" He starts dragging his bleeding body toward the door, but my focus has already switched to her.

It's *all* about her.

I can't stop staring.

Turns out, I was missing the real masterpiece underneath her clothes.

I want her.

I fucking want her.

My gaze drops to the soft mound barely concealed beneath the black lace. *I bet she tastes like peaches and cream...*

She moans suddenly, her head falling to one side—hair strewn like dark seaweed across the flawless shores of her cheek.

Focus, Sam. Focus.

She's the daughter of the enemy. It's Mexico versus

Colombia. It's the past versus our present. It's the fact that her daddy, Valentin Carrera, swore an oath years ago to bring death and destruction to the Santiago Cartel, an organization in which my stepfather is so entrenched, even his shit stinks of South America.

There's bad blood, and then there's this—a war so dangerous it kills people by seven degrees of separation.

She was meant to be my way into Santiago's organization. Mess her up a little. Fuck with her heart. Make everyone pay attention... Truth is, I'm done playing with wooden guns in safe, wooden houses, and being forced into a state of peace and tranquility when my black soul screams for anarchy. My stepfather argues that this war is the parents' fight. That their sins should absolve the next generation from bloodshed.

Screw that.

Not so long ago, he ruled the New York underground for Santiago. Now, I want a piece of his former action, and Santiago, *my godfather*, is the man to give it to me.

Running the edge of my knife across the unblemished plains of Lola's stomach, I follow the curve of her hipbone all the way to the black borderline of her panties. She moans again, and slurs out a word, but her eyes never open.

My lips twitch as an idea forms. The tip of the blade makes a shockingly white indentation before the first bud of crimson blooms.

I work quickly after that—a master of my wicked art—marking the flawless skin just left of her hipbone with a single letter that spans a couple of inches wide, and deep enough to scar.

S for my initial.

S for Santiago.

Rising from the bed, I admire my handiwork. What I've done to her is far worse than what Troy Davis could ever do. I've fucked with her body, and tomorrow that letter will be fucking with her mind.

I've finally announced my intention as a player in this war, but best of all?

I've made Lola Carrera mine.

CHAPTER
Four

LOLA

I wake in my apartment to the sound of my teeth chattering, each clap of enamel chipping away at my brain. Prying my eyes open, I wince at the sharp haze filtering through my lashes.

Fuck, it's bright.

I lift my arm to block out the sunlight, but the damn thing feels like a sack of bricks. Since gravity is waging war against me, I give up, letting it flop back down. *Big mistake.* The moment it lands across the bridge of my nose, I let out a hoarse cry as dozens of sharp knives plunge into my skull.

"What the hell?" My voice is barely audible. *Rough. Brittle.* Like my *Tío* Mateo sounded after taking a bullet to the chest a couple of years ago.

But I didn't get shot. This is New Jersey, not Mexico City.

Blowing out a queasy breath, I dig my elbow into the mattress and sit up, my body accompanying my chattering teeth in a symphony of tremors. When a sudden wave of nausea hits, I swallow hard, unsure if I'm going to black out or vomit all over my bed.

Breathe, Lola.

Dios mío, I must have had more to drink than I thought.

As my spinning head settles, I recall the single Bacardi and Coke I nursed all night. I was reckless, not stupid. I only allowed myself one drink, but I remember stumbling up a flight of stairs and then down a long hallway.

Someone was with me…

Beep! Beep! Beep!

"Argh, fuck!" Grabbing my head to stop the sound of my alarm from shattering my eardrums, I roll over, a sharp pain radiating across my abdomen as I search for my phone. "Shut up!" I growl. Dragging it off the nightstand, I hit all the buttons at once, praying one will stop the incessant noise.

Finally, silence.

Tossing it on the mattress, I flop back onto my pillow, when it hits me.

"Shit! Santi…" *I'm supposed to meet my brother for lunch.* Adrenaline spikes through my veins as I throw my comforter across the bed. It isn't until my feet hit the floor that I realize I'm naked.

Dread fills my chest as I force pieces of last night from behind the distorted opaque window clouding my mind. *How did I get home?*

Slowly, more jagged memories work their way out of the fog and into the light.

No. I couldn't have.

Troy Davis.

His hands.

A bed.

"Trust me, baby. I'm gonna treat this pussy good."

Trust me…

"No…" I breathe again, searching between my legs for signs of my worst fear. But there's no blood on my thighs, and I don't feel violated.

That's when a dark crimson stain catches my eye. The one smeared across the inside of my white comforter. It mocks me, daring me to come closer.

So, I do.

But as I twist toward the stained blanket, I draw in a sharp breath as another stinging pain shoots from my hip. Slowly, I glance down to see what could've caused such an ache.

What I see turns my blood to ice.

I'm bleeding all right, but not from a dick. Midway between my navel and left hip bone, someone carved a letter into my skin.

No, not someone. Troy Davis.

A fucking S.

I scream out in anger and frustration. I don't have to guess what that letter stands for. It speaks for itself.

Slut.

That bastard has no idea what he's done. One word—one *whisper* from me—and I can't count the number of ways he'd suffer, or the pieces of him that would end up scattered across all five boroughs.

And then I'd end up right back in Mexico behind the iron bars I just escaped.

This is why I'll be keeping Troy's assault and desecration to myself, as will every single one of my friends if they know what's good for them.

As far as they know, I'm María Diaz, the child of Cuban immigrants. They smile their plastic smiles, flip their blonde hair, and link arms with me, all while pretending they don't know exactly what I'm capable of.

They do. They just choose to lock it behind their gated suburban lies.

Fear is a deceptive spiritual guide.

Wrapping the sheet around myself, I shove everything away to deal with later. *Always later.* I can't afford to let the great Santi Carrera, my big brother, and the heir apparent of my father's empire, see weakness.

Because God forbid, I have a say in anything.

Santi left me alone in Mexico City two years ago to come to America and take control of our family's New Jersey cocaine distribution. No one asked me what I wanted.

Stay in Mexico and marry a nice boy, Lola.

Well, screw that.

Since my brother left, I've moved heaven and earth to follow him—which includes somehow convincing my overprotective parents to let me attend college in the heart of a warzone.

Making my way to the bathroom, I turn on the shower full blast. Before the water is even hot, I step inside, letting it wash away my sins. Even the ones I don't regret.

At least they were mine to make.

Control and freedom are two words I've craved but have been denied for years. Equal opportunity may be a right in the States, but things aren't so cut and dry where I'm from.

Not that women don't hold power in my world. I'm just not part of that exclusive club.

I'm Valentin Carrera's daughter. The king's innocent *cielito*—his little sky. I'm much too fragile to be tainted by the blood staining the hands of every member of my family. *Ay Dios mío*, I couldn't even cross the border and go to college without two huge bodyguards and my brother lurking behind every damn tree.

Maybe that's why I did it.

After stepping out of the shower, my mind spins like a Tilt-a-Whirl as I rush to throw on a pair of loose-fitting shorts and the least wrinkled shirt I can find.

I bite my lip while towel-drying my hair. My rebellion last night was stupid, but exhilarating. I've kept a low profile since arriving on campus, so when my friend, Avery, suggested we blow off some steam, I was all in.

Party? *Hell yeah.* Booze? *Bring it.* Rich boys? *Even better.*

Then she said *his* name.

Sam Colton.

Slipping on a pair of sandals, I grab my phone and car keys and rush out the door, my hangover and stinging skin already forgotten. Instead, my head fills with a pair of watchful dark eyes.

Eyes so black I'm not sure there's a beginning or end. *Just infinite night.*

Taking the stairs two at a time, I keep a check on the time as I race across the parking lot toward my white BMW. I'm halfway there when a cool breeze licks down the back of my neck, causing my steps to falter.

My father's words ring like a church bell in my ears.

Always trust your instincts, cielito.

"Is someone there?"

Of course, no one answers. The majority of the campus is still sleeping away their hangovers. Still, my feet refuse to move, cemented to the ground by a fatal curiosity.

I know all about the statistics of campus assault. I'm a prime target.

Young girl alone...

No one around to hear her cries for help...

It's a thought that should terrify me, but it doesn't. *It excites me.* There's something familiar in the air. Something forbidden and dangerous yet tantalizing and enticing.

Tightening my hold around the key fob, I hover my thumb over the panic button. "That's it," I mutter, shaking my head. "No more alcohol."

After settling behind the wheel, I lock the door and let out an unsettled breath. I can't shake the feeling I'm being watched.

Stalked.

Hunted.

As if my every move is a choreographed step in someone else's dance.

"You're losing it, Carrera." Starting the ignition, I turn to back out of the parking spot, when the wound on my stomach stings under the crude bandage I fashioned earlier. The corners of my mouth turn down, my momentary euphoria tanking at the bleak reminder.

I should've suggested we go to another party, but I didn't. Even though I knew better. Even though I've been cautioned.

"Stay away from Sam Colton, chaparrita. He's dangerous."

I rolled my eyes when my brother issued his warning. How could the hottest, most popular boy on campus be the most hazardous to my health? What the hell did he know about him that I didn't?

Temptation is a baited trap. Last night, I crept closer, knowing the second I touched the forbidden treat, a hair trigger would snap my neck.

But there's something about him... Something so mesmerizing it's worth the risk.

Danger is the most addictive drug, and Sam has me hooked.

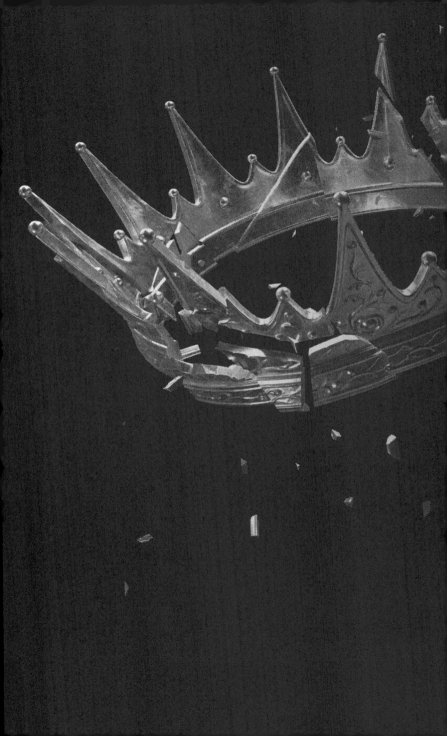

CHAPTER
Five

LOLA

"Not hungry?" My brother raises an eyebrow at me from across the small table.

I glance down at my untouched plate. "I don't like pizza."

Ugh, why did he have to pick an Italian restaurant? Thanks to our father, he has more money than all of New Jersey combined, yet here we sit in some godawful strip mall pizzeria.

"Bullshit. That ham and pineapple stuff is your favorite."

My stomach lurches. "Santi, please." I place my napkin on my plate, and *gracias a Dios*, it blocks the layer of grease from sight. "Will you lay off already?"

"No." He tosses me a lethal smirk.

I scrunch my nose in disgust. If we weren't in a public place, I'd punch it right off his face. Instead, I glare at him. "I'm sick, all right?" Crossing my arms, I slump into my chair. "I think I have the flu."

"You smell like last call." My big brother leans forward, the gold flecks in his eyes glinting with accusation. "The only thing you *have* is a hangover." I jump as he slams his palm onto the table. "What have I told you about the consequences of drinking around strangers?"

"That I could have fun?"

Santi's hand clenches, the vein in his temple pulsing with every grind of his teeth.

Christ, he's the spitting image of papá.

"You're testing me, *chaparrita*," he warns darkly.

I cringe at his childhood nickname for me. *Shorty.*

"You might get hurt," he continues, pausing on a slow inhale. "Where did you go last night? Felipé is getting his balls chopped off because of you."

My jaw drops. "What? Why?"

His eyes flash with an unforgiving truth no border walls can contain. "He's one of your personal guards, Lola. *Papá's* direct link to you besides me. What did you think would happen when you ditched him last night?"

Oh shit.

That's just it; I *didn't* think. Our father is merciless enough, but when it comes to me, he's inhuman. For some reason, I flip a switch in him that even *mamá* can't control.

Felipé is a pain in my ass, but he doesn't deserve *papá's* wrath.

"I'll call *papá*." I reach for my phone, my hands shaking so badly, I nearly knock over my water. "I'll tell him it was my"—I draw in a sharp breath as the tender flesh beside my hip burns—"my fault," I finish weakly. Keeping my gaze lowered, I try to pull up my father's coded contact in my phone.

Why won't my hand stop shaking?

I'm not afforded another attempt. Santi's bronzed one darts across the table and clamps on top of mine. "That's not how it works, and you know it. Actions have consequences. Unfortunately, Felipé will pay for yours."

I nod. It makes me sick to my stomach, but he's right. This is the way of our world, and no amount of pleading will change it.

As the pressure on my hand releases, I jerk my phone to my chest. *Bad move.* White, hot, pain tears through my body like a greased bobsled.

"Something's wrong."

It's not a question.

"Yeah." I wince, shifting in my chair. "Our father is about to castrate a man, and I'm about to throw up my spleen. Not a good day for vital organs."

Awesome, Lola. Crack a joke. That's always helpful.

He ignores my insolence. "Every time you move, you wince and clench your fists. You're hurt, so I'll ask again. Where were you last night?" He jabs a finger at me from across the table. "And don't lie to me."

"I sort of had a date." *Technically, it's not so much a lie as a bent truth.* "It didn't go so well."

"What does that mean?"

"He gave me a drink, and then it's all a big blur."

Santi's restrained anger explodes, his palms smacking the table again as his feet hit the floor. Glasses rattle and tip over, shattering into serrated pieces. "You deliberately put yourself in a vulnerable situation, opening the door for some asshole to roofie you? Of all the stupid—"

The entire restaurant falls silent as eyes shift toward us. This is the last thing either of us needs. "Santi," I plead in a low tone. "Please don't. Not here."

His gaze shifts to the left before he slowly sinks back into his seat. But I don't take my eyes off him. Just because the dragon isn't roaring, that doesn't mean he's not still breathing fire.

"Name," he says flatly.

"Santi…"

"Name, *chaparrita*. Don't make me seek it out myself." He issues the threat calmly, his nostrils flaring like a raging bull. "You won't like what happens."

I believe him.

"Troy Davis."

Santi pulls out his phone, and within seconds, he has someone on the line. "It's Carrera. Find a student named Troy Davis. Bring him to the docks and then wait for me there." Without another word, he disconnects the call and pockets his phone.

"What are you going to do?"

He holds my stare for one too many skipped heartbeats before speaking again, his tone dangerously calm. "You're a Carrera, Lola. You should know better than to let your guard down. Do you know how many men in this town would take a blade to you just to get to me? To get to *papá*?"

"No worries. Troy already took care of that," I mutter.

His eyes narrow into deadly slits. "Show me."

"*Here*? No!"

"I won't ask twice. You can show me, or I'll have RJ show me." He tilts his head to his left, where our cousin, Santi's second-in-command, sits watching our every move.

So that's who he was looking at.

"You wouldn't dare," I hiss, calling his bluff.

"Try me."

"You let him anywhere near me, and *papá* will shove a gun so far up your ass, you'll be burping bullets."

His full lips tip into a disturbing smile. "You think *papá* won't sanction my commands? Think again, *chaparrita*. I'm king in this state. You're just the kid who ditched her guard, went to a Santiago-affiliated party, and got herself roofied."

I glare at him, refusing his request, when his words blaze through my mind, leaving a scorched trail of deceit. "Wait, a *what* party?"

"Exactly," he scolds, folding his arms, his biceps straining beneath his white button-up shirt. "You have no idea the danger you've put yourself and this family in."

His accusation is like a punch to the chest. "I don't understand. How?"

Of course, he doesn't answer my question. He never does. This is Santi Carrera's world; we just live in it.

"Show me," he repeats, his jaw clenched.

Cursing under my breath, I tap the camera icon on my phone with more force than necessary.

"What are you doing?"

"Giving you what you asked for." As discreetly as possible, I lift the hem of my shirt and lower the elastic waistband on my shorts, quickly snapping a picture. Gritting my teeth, I shove my hand across the table. "They say a picture's worth a thousand words... Well, how about a letter?" I snort at my own joke as he takes my phone. "The bastard gave me a scarlet one.

He carved an S for slut right next to my hip."

My heart stutters as fire sweeps up my brother's neck, igniting an all too familiar bloodlust in his eyes.

"It's not that bad," I whisper, shrinking into my seat. "Once it heals, I'll get a tattoo over it. It won't even show."

"The S is not for slut," he says in a clipped tone.

A few precious beats pass...

And then all hell breaks loose.

Santi stands, his expensive Santoni dress shoes hitting the tiles seconds before a roar rips from his chest. Flipping the table, he sends it flying across the restaurant and then storms out the door.

What the hell just happened?

I glance toward RJ, who simply shrugs and pulls a wad of bills from his pocket.

Oh, for fuck's sake...

It's not smart or rational, but I follow after my brother. It only takes a couple of steps to spot him leaning against the side of a building, a newly lit cigarette hanging from his lips.

By the time I reach him, I'm more than a little pissed off myself. "What the hell is wrong with you? And since when do you smoke?"

A little hypocritical, but whatever.

"Since about thirty seconds ago—right about the time I realized my sister started the next phase of this war."

"What's that supposed to mean?"

Leaving the burning embers tucked between his lips, he pulls his phone from his pocket and scrolls until he finds what he's looking for. Taking a long drag, he pulls the cigarette out of his mouth and holds up a picture. "Look familiar?"

My knees nearly buckle. *No.* That can't be right.

"Who's that?"

"Nora, my dock hand, who I compensated very well to clear all my shipments. She was on my payroll." He taps his middle finger against the rectangular thing lying beneath her. "Now she's on a metal slab at the medical examiner's office. A Carrera associate was about to perform her autopsy when he sent me this photo." He jabs the same finger toward the center of the screen, "And that, dear sister, is the same scarlet letter carved into her chest."

I can't breathe.

"S isn't for slut, Lola. It's for Santiago."

Breathe. Just breathe.

Dropping the barely-smoked cigarette onto the pavement, Santi stomps it out with the heel of his shoe while shoving his phone back into his pocket. "I told you to stay the fuck away from Colton."

"I have! What's he got to do with this anyway?"

"*Mamá.*"

The word is like another deep cut to my skin. Our father has sheltered me from most inner workings of the family business, save one. *Mamá's* role in the eighteen-year Carrera/ Santiago feud is something that even the great Valentin Carrera could never hide.

Not when the ripple effect lasted well into our childhood.

A temporary alliance between Dante Santiago and my father turned into a third-party massacre at my *Tía* Adriana and *Tío* Brody's wedding. My mother, pregnant with me at the time, got caught in the line of fire, and it nearly killed both of us.

Papá laid the blame at Dante Santiago's feet, swearing vengeance against his cartel and its bloodline.

I shake my head. "But that has to do with the Santiago Cartel, and Sam—"

"Colton *is* the Santiago Cartel," he says coldly. "He's operating under a false name, *María*." I wince at his mocking drawl of my alias. "His real last name is Sanders, otherwise known as Senator Rick Sanders's stepson. You know, the former New York kingpin turned politician? Santiago *owns* New York," he stresses, shoving a hand through his thick, dark hair. "*Dios mío*, Lola!"

The way he spits out my name, it might as well be another curse word.

"How could *I* have known that?" I insist, my voice shaking as I defend myself. "You and *papá* don't tell me anything!"

"You weren't on a date last night," he accuses, taking two steps toward me. "You were with *him*. ¡*No me mientas!* Don't lie to me." His bitter expression turns deadly as he backs me against the building. "Right now, Troy Davis is being dragged from his hospital bed and will soon be chained to a metal beam. I'm already going to shred him into unrecognizable ribbons of flesh. It's your call whether his death will be quick or drawn out."

We stare at each other, my voice trapped in my throat.

"It'd be a shame if he endured unnecessary torture while paying for someone else's sins," he adds viciously.

My stomach lurches. "Fine! I was at Sam Colton's…" At Santi's dipped chin, I clench my teeth. "I mean Sam *Sanders's* party, but I swear Troy *did* put something in my drink. The last thing I remember is him taking me upstairs."

I force myself not to cringe as Troy's foreboding whispers from last night slithers through a hazy crack in my memory. *Trust me...*

My brother's eyes are crazed with hate as he draws his arm back and drives his fist into the wall. I cringe at the sickening sound.

"Sam didn't touch me, Santi!" I scream, looking up at him with pleading eyes. "We've never even spoken to each other." *Words as painful as they are accurate.*

I've never had to fight for a man's attention, but at that party, I'd locked gazes with him. I'd bitten my bottom lip, letting it slowly slide through my teeth.

Teasing him...

Enticing him...

And then nothing.

For a man who couldn't take his eyes off me, he sure as hell couldn't take a hint.

I never even wanted Troy Davis.

Guess the joke's on me.

"You think he didn't touch you?" A tight frown tugs at the corners of Santi's mouth. "Are you sure about that, *chaparrita*?" Cupping my chin, he leans close. "*This* is why *papá* didn't want you in America. You're too innocent. Too fucking trusting." His eyes flash with a hint of sadness as he pushes off the wall and walks away.

"Where are you going?" I call after him.

"To clean up your mess."

"Santi!"

He pauses but doesn't turn around. "You're my baby sister, Lola. *A Carrera*. By touching you, Sanders fired the first shot."

I wince at the ruthlessness in his voice. "What are you going to do?"

"Fire the last."

CHAPTER
Six

SAM

The table flips.

Pizza goes flying in all directions.

Blind rage heads for the front door, with sweet confusion trailing after him.

Flexing my grip, I loosen the gun's connection with the back of the guard's head as I glance at another security feed that shows Santi Carrera slamming his fist into the wall outside the restaurant.

"Expand on camera three," I order, and the terrified strip mall guard complies with shaking fingers. Within seconds, the main screen is a forty-six-inch display of satisfaction.

Some say it's an unparalleled feeling when your blade penetrates deep into the heart of your enemy. For me, their reaction is even better. The look on Carrera's face right now is more stunning than a sunset over the Grand Canyon.

It's a brief euphoria, though.

The dark clouds roll in the moment he takes Lola's chin. *The moment he touches what's mine.*

"P-please, don't hurt me."

I glance down to see that I've rammed the muzzle of my gun into the guard's head so hard his face is bowed over a keyboard.

"You've done well," I say, easing up on the contact again. "Don't ruin it. Tell anyone I was here, and you're a dead man." Tossing a couple of hundred-dollar bills onto the desk next to him, I drop my gun and exit the security booth.

By the time I reach my Bugatti, Lola is on the move. I placed a tracking device on her white BMW the night she switched my world to monotone. The moment she made it all about *her.*

Glancing at my cell, I watch her take a right. My lips curve into a smile.

So pretty.

So predictable.

I know exactly where she's headed—my apartment. She wants to raise hell about what I did last night, but I'll always be one step ahead. Once she reaches her destination, I have a fun surprise in store for her.

Lola, Lola, Lola.

She burns as bright as the sun, and I can never get enough.

Pulling out of the parking lot myself, I set a course for the opposite direction. If I can't have her body, I'll satisfy myself with the next best thing.

Twenty minutes later, I'm parking outside her apartment. I kill the block's security feed with a swipe of my finger. My phone starts beeping as I'm reaching the front door.

My office. Two hours.

I expected this. The senator has eyes and ears all over the East Coast. It was only a matter of time before I was dragged before his court of reckoning. *Well, guess what, stepdaddy dearest? I have a little reckoning of my own to toss around.*

Her apartment smells of her.

I cut a trail down the hallway, through her bedroom and into her bathroom. I run my finger over her bottles of perfumes and moisturizers, shampoos and conditioners. I find her birth control tablets stashed at the back of the vanity unit and force myself not to pop out every little yellow pill and crush them beneath the heel of my sneakers.

The idea of my child growing inside her turns my dick to stone.

My child.

No one else's…

Fuck.

Kids?

I'm driving myself insane with these thoughts. I'm only twenty years old. I can have any woman I want, but no one else can satisfy me like she can.

I want to use her.

Complete her.

Dirty up her tongue.

Stain her insides.

Spread her perfect ass cheeks and lavish attention on the most secret part of her.

Hissing out a curse, I fall against the vanity unit—gripping the white porcelain basin with one hand as I tear at my zipper with the other. Tipping my head back, I fill my lungs with her scent and her ghost as I work my cock like a man possessed.

Longing.

Needing.

Hard, for the diamond edges of this insatiable lust.

Fast, for how quick this descent into her madness has become.

My wrist aches.

My cock swells.

I groan in pain and elation as lightning zips down my spine and my balls draw tight to my body. I shoot my load so violently, thick ropes of it streak across the porcelain, blemishing the polished silver faucet and mirror.

With my head still swimming, I clean myself up and head for the door. I don't bother wiping away my sin. This won't be the last time I corrupt a part of Lola Carrera. As long as there's breath in *my* body, no other man will take their pleasure from hers.

My phone beeps again as I slip out of her apartment and make my way down the exit stairway to the parking lot.

You're in deep shit, Sam. Care to make it an abyss? I told you to stay away from her. My office. Time is ticking.

Despite my stepfather's fighting words, I'm in a conciliatory mood as I slide into the driver's seat. After checking Lola's car tracker and seeing she's headed home, I tap out a brief response.

On my way.

It's high time the senator had a lesson in generational deposition.

There's a new Sanders in town, and he better get used to it.

CHAPTER
Seven

LOLA

I shouldn't warn him.

I should go back to my apartment and let Santi dish out whatever punishment he sees fit. After all, Troy tried to rape me, and Sam...

Oh my God, did he brand me?

We've never said two words to each other before, but it seems he's happy to let his knife do the talking. I thought the new blood thrumming through the veins of the cartel underworld might dilute this feud between our families. Instead, it seems to have fortified it. Fueled it. Twisted it into something much darker...

Now, instead of standing on the outskirts of war, I've been forced across its borders and made into a casualty.

I shouldn't warn him.

The words repeat in my head as I pull my car into the

parking lot outside his apartment. They burrow deep into my psyche as I climb the pretentious marble steps leading to his front door. They slice into my heart as I reach out a shaking finger and ring the doorbell.

Nothing.

I ring it again.

Nothing.

"Sam?" I press my face against the narrow window beside the door. There doesn't appear to be any movement, but I still call his name. "I know you're in there, Sam *Sanders*," I say, hissing the now-familiar last name. "You don't know who the hell you've messed with. Why don't you come out here and face me now that I'm conscious?"

Nothing.

Shit.

Exhaustion and nerves hit all at once, and I collapse forward, dropping my forehead against the glass. Heaving a sigh, I twist around until my back hits the brick wall next to it.

Nice. Real smooth, Lola.

I have no idea what I'm doing. I came here with no plan and no forethought. All I know is that I can't get Santi's words out of my head.

"Sam didn't touch me, Santi! We've never even spoken to each other."

"Are you sure about that, chaparrita?"

I thought I was. But now I can't seem to remember much of anything. And if Santi is right, and this S carved on me stands for Santiago, at some point late last night, I was alone with Colton.

Sanders...*whatever.*

Something dark and forbidden flares inside me. Something I can never speak of or acknowledge. The thought of him touching me should sicken me, but it doesn't.

Quite the opposite.

"It's just the drugs," I say with a groan, stepping away from the apartment. "Whatever Troy slipped in my drink messed up my head." Sighing, I turn to leave, when a piece of yellow paper stuck to the far side of the door catches my eye.

The closer I get, I realize it's a Post-it Note that someone has scribbled on. Ripping it off the door, I read it word for word and line for line. Then I read it twice more as a rush of heat crawls up my neck and stains my face.

When I read his words for the fourth time, I swear I can feel him watching me again.

My mouse doesn't want to be caught. Unless that's what she desires most... Better luck next time, dulzura.

CHAPTER
Eight

SAM

S enator Rick Sanders doesn't raise his voice.

Even as a kid, growing up with my twin half-brother and sister, I can't recall a single time he yelled at us.

His methods of showing his displeasure are far more refined. When he's really pissed, like he is now, his gray eyes darken to cold steel and the sharp lines of his Armani suit take on all the comfort of razor blades.

It's his tone that chills the most. His easy drawl drops to a low and vicious rasp where every word, every vowel, *every inflection* returns to the tough Brooklyn streets where he grew up.

"What the fuck did you do last night, Sam?"

"You know exactly what I did, Daddio, and you know why I did it."

Leaning back in my chair, I gaze unseeingly at the white

architrave in his five-million-dollar penthouse home office. My bodyguard-jailers work for him, not me, so I knew a call to the senator would have been made the moment Lola Carrera walked into my party.

Still, they have their uses. Tapping phones is another trick I learned before my eighth birthday. After that, I graduated fast. These days, there isn't a computer system I can't hack, which is how I know my worth to an organization like Santiago's.

Did she find the note yet?

"Nina is angry with you as well."

"Why?" I say, dropping my head. "She's not my mother. The first Mrs. Sanders is pushing up thorns in Calvary Cemetery, remember?"

So is my piece of shit, deadbeat dad if we're skipping down that happy trail. He was found with his throat slit the day Rick discovered I wasn't his. My stepfather doesn't like loose ends.

"Manners, Sam," he murmurs, his subtext clear. *Stop acting like a dick.*

I can't help it, even though I actually think my stepfather is pretty cool.

"You're just a kid playing in an adult world with very adult rules." The senator fixes me with a glare, and I return it with a grin.

"Are you jealous, Daddio? Before my stepmother came along, you'd screwed half of Manhattan's trophy wives, plus their mothers-in-law."

At this, there's a deep rumble of laughter behind me—a slow, dangerous, sleeper of a sound that hits me like a freight train.

Spinning around, I see the tall, inimitable, scary-as-hell figure of my godfather darkening up the doorway.

"The boy has your mouth, Sanders," he says, striding toward us. *Black jeans. Black shirt.* It's kind of fitting after all the death he's dealt in the last fifty years. "I believe the nature versus nurture debate just got resolved."

"Go fuck yourself, Dante," my stepfather drawls, seemingly unsurprised by the Colombian kingpin's appearance. He tosses a couple of photographs across the desk at him. "Turns out we share the same exquisite taste in women."

I catch a sideways glance, and my stomach drops. They're all of Lola from last night, approximately thirty minutes before Troy exited stage left at a bloody crawl.

The senator laughs when he notices the look on my face. "We expected you to screw her, not brand her, you stupid dickhead."

Wait, what?

"You're not pissed at what I did?" I say, frowning in confusion.

His eyes glint in amusement. "You've had your fun, Sam... Let's just say I wanted in on the action. Christ, you're even more belligerent than I am when backed into a corner."

What the hell is going on here?

"Does Santiago know who she is?"

"*Santiago* knew the moment she graced American soil," my godfather interrupts, cocking a dark eyebrow at me. "When my enemy's daughter happens to sweet-talk her way out of her heavily-armed Mexican compound and within touching distance of my territory, it would be remiss of me *not* to welcome her in with open arms."

Before I crush her with them.

I fill in that last part for myself.

"You played me, Daddio." Shades of red start misting up my vision. I hate being blindsided. *I hate that I don't have a plan in place to take the heat off their interest in her.*

But I will.

Because Lola is mine, not theirs.

"Reverse psychology, Sammio," he says, handing my own mockery back to me, fighting another grin. "Tell the cool kid to stay away from the hot new chick on campus, then watch the sparks fly."

"It was a test."

"A test," he confirms.

"You never had any issues about me working for Santiago."

"Sam," he says with a sigh. "I'd be the last fucking prick to lecture you about blurred lines and morality, but if you're planning to dance on the wrong side of the law, I'd prefer it if you partnered up with us. Edier Grayson is poised to take control of New York, and we want you as his second."

"You stepped in when it mattered most." I can feel Dante's dark eyes punching a hole in my face as he interjects. "I can't exact revenge on a body that's already damaged."

I know what he's talking about right away.

"Troy Davis." There's a pause. "Is he dead?"

"He will be soon, but not by my hand. Carrera got to him first. If it were one of my daughters he'd drugged and assaulted, there wouldn't be much of him left."

The look on his face sends a shiver through my body. *You don't fuck with this man and get to swap stories about it.*

He gestures at the bar in the corner. "Bourbon, Sanders."

"Get it yourself," comes the easy riposte.

"The knife in the quarterback's leg was a nice touch." I watch, heart hammering, as the Colombian helps himself to my stepfather's liquor. "Remind me to use it on the next Carrera we torture."

"But not Lola."

I say it too fast.

Too obvious.

"No, not Lola." He shoots me a look over the rim of his glass. "I have more creative designs on her than that. Even more creative than carving my initial into her skin."

I don't correct his assumption. Even though that letter, *that body*, belongs to me, not him.

I point to the photos on the desk. "Tell me what you're planning to do to her."

The temperature in the room drops sharply.

"That sounded dangerously close to an order," Dante says idly. "Can you spell the word respect, or would you like my fist to give you a lesson?"

"Let it go, Santiago," my stepfather warns. "There's no dick swinging in my office unless it's mine and my wife is doing the honors."

"Stay close to her." He finishes up his drink and pours himself another. "We arranged for her brother, Santi, to be out of town last night, but we won't be that lucky again for a while."

"Since when do you take such a keen interest in my sex life?" I say, losing my cool.

"Since the moment you flashed up on Lola Carrera's radar," Dante clips back. "She sees you, Sam... And when a cartel princess *sees*, she doesn't usually stop until she *gets*." He slams his glass down, that wicked smirk catching at the corners of his mouth again. "That's when you make things interesting. That's when there's no crueler torture than a bleeding heart."

CHAPTER
Nine

LOLA

My concentration is shot to hell.

After the fourth time scanning the same paragraph, I slam my social sciences book closed and toss it away. Groaning, I press my fingers against my closed eyelids as I sit cross-legged in the middle of my bed.

I have no clue what I just read.

Although, I shouldn't be shocked—there's no room left inside my head for useless information. I thought keeping busy the rest of the day would occupy all the space he's claimed, but that's an impossible feat.

Especially when it's just as marked with his name as my skin.

Even after eight hours of senseless shopping and a caffeine-infused coffee-house crawl, I still can't get Sam, or his dark note, off my mind.

My elbows dig into the inside of my knees as I slump forward. Sinking my fingers into my hair, I tug at the strands as if somehow it will unroot memories from last night.

The ones of him.

The ones of him touching me.

Marking me.

Seeing me.

He witnessed me at my most vulnerable—naked and at his mercy. He could have added his enemy's innocence to his claims last night, but he didn't.

Why?

And why the hell am I even questioning it?

I should be counting my blessings that last night only cost me a physical scar. It could have been much worse. He could have left me with plenty more that would never heal.

Digging into the pocket of my shorts, I pull out a crumpled yellow piece of paper, my heart leaping into my throat as I smooth it out on my bare thigh.

My mouse doesn't want to be caught. Unless that's what she desires most... Better luck next time, dulzura.

Dulzura.

Sweetness? What the hell is that? I'm sure it wasn't meant as a term of endearment as much as a well-aimed dart. Just like all Santiagos, he managed to twist something innocent into something dark and perverted.

I should be furious. Instead, I want to twist back.

Which would be suicidal.

Sandwiching the Post-it Note between my palms, I press them against my lips almost as if in prayer. For what, I have no idea.

Forgiveness for my sins?

Strength not to commit more?

Wisdom to know the damn difference?

Sam Sanders... Just his name should be a cold slap of reality. If knowledge is power, then knowing who Sam Colton really is should drown this infatuation in a deep pool of vengeance.

So why don't I hate him?

Why do I still have his note?

Two more questions I don't have the answers to.

Unfolding my legs, I climb off my bed, wondering just how high this ledge is... The one I seem to have found myself cornered on with nowhere to run. No means of escape.

No way out but straight down.

Moving toward the window, I brush the curtain with the back of my hand. Unsurprisingly, my only view is a steel jaw and tense, folded arms. It's dark, but then again, so is RJ. I wouldn't be surprised if he bribes the sun just to exist in its light.

The streetlight casts a demonic glow across his expressionless face. He's not in a pleasant mood, and with good reason. I had him chasing me all over New Brunswick today like we were two rats in a bullet-ridden maze.

Courtesy of one overprotective future cartel king.

"Well played, Santi," I mutter.

My brother is nothing if not shrewd. My father has already punished one of my trusted bodyguards for my actions—RJ is his calculated replacement.

Slumping against the window frame, I let out a weary sigh. I never intentionally meant to cause Felipé harm. He was a good bodyguard. A good *sicario*. A good man. But in cartel life, good and bad are simply varying shades of the same intent—*loyalty*.

Felipé wasn't family.

But RJ is...

Santi knows damn well I'd never do anything impulsive and risk our cousin's life—*like ditch him to go to an enemy's party*.

The thought barely takes form in my head before he lifts his chin and meets my stare head-on. *Yep, he's pissed...* RJ doesn't smirk or sneer. He just continues to stare up at me, his arms pulled tightly across his white button-up as he leans up against the hood of his car.

He'd be a lot more pissed if he knew I saw him at that restaurant in North Caldwell a week ago. From what I witnessed, it seems I'm not the only one with my ass on the line.

Sighing, I pull my hand back and the curtain flutters back into place. *A caged princess with no prince in sight.* The Post-it Note feels like a tangle of thorns in my hand as I collapse against the wall.

Why the hell did I go to his place to try and warn him? That's a direct betrayal of not only my brother, but my entire family.

Because the thought of Sam getting hurt terrifies you, a voice in my head answers.

Which makes zero sense. The man has done nothing but play mind games with me, yet here I am...

Protecting him.

I push away from the window.

No. I'm stronger than this.

Balling the note, I toss it in the trash can next to my nightstand. "You're wrong, Sam," I promise under my breath. "This is one mouse you'll never catch."

Flopping back onto my bed, I reach for my textbook, when my phone rings. One glance at the caller ID, and I contemplate sending it straight to voicemail. I'm in no mood to play identity roulette right now. However, ever since arriving in America, I've learned there are two truths in life: I'll never escape my name, and Avery Thorpe will not be ignored.

Swiping the damn thing off the nightstand, I force pleasantries I don't feel. "Hi, Ave…"

"It's about damn time."

"Yeah, sorry about that." I glance toward the window, where I know RJ still sits on the other side, brooding. "I had a lot of studying to do."

"It's Saturday." Before I can come up with a suitable rebuttal, she adds, "And that's bullshit. You haven't been home all day—we checked."

Shit.

"Look, I—"

"Spill, Diaz," she interrupts. "I want all the horny details."

My grip tightens around my phone. "What?"

"Troy…you lucky bitch. We all saw you go upstairs with him last night at the party. We looked for you later on, but someone said you'd left with him."

I wince. *I left…but not with Troy.*

"Someone saw wrong," I say flatly.

I might as well have said someone saw me sprout horns and a tail and then screw Satan on the hood of Sam's Bugatti.

"Own it, María. Hell, I'd tattoo that shit on my forehead

if I were you."

I roll my eyes. "That'd make for an awkward job interview."

She laughs, a sound which slices through the thick tension that's been wrapped around me since meeting with Santi.

Rubbing my temple, I exhale a breath that's half-sigh and half-laugh. "Nothing happened, Avery. I turned him down, so he ditched me and hung around for a while."

Technically, it's not a lie. If Santi has had his way, Troy is probably doing a lot of hanging.

"I slept in my own bed last night...alone," I add, intercepting what I know to be a forthcoming assumption.

Again, technically not a lie.

"Whatever," she mutters. "We'll get it out of you tonight after a few drinks."

Wait, what?

"Tonight?"

"Don't tell me you forgot. Girls night?" When I don't say anything, she groans out her annoyance. "We planned it weeks ago."

Which is exactly why I forgot about it.

I've never had "girl" friends. I've never had many friends, period. Bearing the Carrera name doesn't lend itself to many sleepovers. This whole "sisterhood" thing is as foreign to me as America itself.

"I'll have to pass." I'm not in a partying mood after just getting roofied, plus Santi would lose his shit—and then pretty blonde girls become dead ones.

"Come on," she whines. "You owe it to us after ditching us last night."

What am I supposed to say to that? It's not like I can tell her the truth. So to avoid any more questions and another possible homicide, I relent.

"Fine." Drawing out the word with a groan, I crane my arm and snag a pen off my nightstand. "Where do I meet you?"

Damn it, I need something to write on. I scan my room, but besides my textbook, there's only one thing in sight.

One taunting piece of discarded yellow paper.

Swinging my legs off the side of the mattress, I clench my teeth as I hook my foot over the rim of the trashcan and then drag it toward me. Begrudgingly, I retrieve the crumpled Post-it Note, smoothing it out and then flipping it over, all while trying not to think about the lethal promise scrawled on the other side.

"The Foxhole, ten o'clock." she says as an engine revs in the background. "And María...?"

"Yeah?"

"Dress to kill."

I stiffen as the line goes dead. Slowly, I turn the Post-it Note back over, re-reading my enemy's words as a graphic warning flares inside my head.

"That's what I'm worried about," I whisper softly.

I stare at my reflection in the bathroom mirror, a horrified expression looking back at me. One sliced into a distorted, crude mosaic crafted by *him*.

His scent lingers somewhere deep in my subconscious. A vicious haven of leather and barbed wire.

One foot moves in front of the other until I'm pressed up against the counter. Reaching forward, I touch the glass, trailing my finger along the dried stains.

I may be a virgin, but I'm not totally innocent. I know what the hell is all over my mirror.

And basin.

And faucets.

Cum.

"You son of a bitch," I hiss, dropping my hand and clenching my fists by my side. Only the words lack conviction. There's no offense entwined with my insult, only fire.

The wrong kind.

I'm furious he invaded my apartment. I'm fearful of how he did it so easily.

But most of all, I'm turned on.

I don't know what game Sam's playing, but it has taken a dangerous turn. He's marked me, and now he's marked the one place I call my own. It's a message I should return with a lipstick-kissed bullet, but I can't ignore the coiling in my belly or the unbearable ache between my legs.

Thoughts of him consume me as carnal need takes over. I close my eyes, diluted justification swimming behind them as my hand slides inside the waistband of my shorts. *It will almost be like we came together…*

Sam…

However, the moment my finger slides in between my wet folds, my eyes fly open in horror. *This is what he wants…* Pissed, I jerk my hand out of my shorts, the elastic waistband snapping back into place with a pop.

No. I won't give him the satisfaction.

"Nice try, asshole." Bending down, I open a cabinet door under the counter, swinging it hard against the wooden base. Armed with a towel in one hand and Windex in the other, I go to erase every trace of him...and then I freeze.

Because some messed-up, masochistic part of me doesn't want to.

Common sense tells me I'm taking a dangerous risk by leaving it there, but logic isn't in control right now—lust is.

Sighing out a frustrated breath, I drop the towel and my clothes into a pile on the bathroom floor. I don't care about the consequences as I turn the shower on full blast and step under a waterfall of scalding hot punishment.

As I lather, images of Sam force their way into my head. His hand pumping his thick cock. His face twisted in Machiavellian pleasure while coming with my name on his lips.

My hand creeps lower.

No, Lola. Don't do it.

I grit my teeth, forcing my hand back up my body, wincing as my fingers graze my still tender hip. Blinking water from my eyes, I glance down at the letter he carved into my skin. I trace the jagged curve that starts at the top, following down its forbidden path.

"S isn't for slut, Lola. It's for Santiago."

The words are sharp shards of ice driven straight into my chest.

Did he do it out of hate, or was it something darker?

"Damn you, Sanders..." Quickly rinsing off, I slam my hand onto the faucet and turn the water off.

Why do I let him get to me like this?

Shoving my hand against the shower door, I drag the discarded towel off the floor and wrap it around my body, not bothering to dry off first.

And then I see it again...

His salacious calling card.

Ripping the towel off, I stomp toward the glass and scrub the mirror and basin until they're both spotless. Taking slow, ragged breaths to diffuse my anger, I hastily shake out the towel and wrap it back around my dripping skin.

It's only then that I realize what I've done.

So much for getting clean. I just coated myself in my stalker's cum.

Wandering back into my bedroom, I open my closet, revealing row after row of designer dresses. However, only one catches my eye.

Dress to kill...

Swallowing any lingering reservation, I reach for the one I know with every fiber of my being I shouldn't wear.

Short, shiny, and silver.

I hope Sam Sanders has the good sense to stay away tonight.

Otherwise, those words may be prophetic.

CHAPTER
Ten

LOLA

The line is already three drunks deep by the time I make my way to the bar. Alcohol is the last thing I should have right now, but my liver is the least of my worries. I need something eighty-proof to get me through the night.

After a few unproductive moments of waiting my turn, I take matters into my own hands. Paying little attention to the dirty looks being shot my way, I push through the crowd and squeeze into a small pocket toward the front.

A bartender, who looks like he just stepped off the pages of an underwear ad, pauses in front of me. "What can I get for you?"

I don't hesitate. "A shot of *Añejo* tequila."

If I'm going to play a king's game, I might as well drink like one.

He lifts an eyebrow. "You got an ID hidden in the dress

somewhere?"

My smile is anything but sweet. Reaching into my bra, I pull out the fake ID Avery and I bought our first week on campus and hand it to him. I'd like to tell him where he can shove it, but I've already landed myself on Santi's radar enough as it is.

He barely even looks at it before tossing it back and turning to face the wall of liquor bottles behind him. While I wait, I scan the perimeter, looking for Avery and the rest of my friends in the sea of shadowed faces.

Nothing.

Damn it.

I have no idea why it was so imperative we come here tonight. The Foxhole isn't anything special. It's just your typical nightclub—thirty-five hundred square feet of chrome acting as reflectors for the magenta and purple stage lights.

And in case one inch of space missed the cotton candy colored memo, the disco ball hanging in the center of the dance floor is there to drive the point home.

Jesus, where'd that guy go to pour my drink—Mexico?

I'm leaning over the bar, trying to see where he could've gone, when I feel a hand grab my ass from behind.

"What the hell?" I spin around, nearly tumbling into another pretentious polo shirt stretched across a broad chest.

Ay Dios mío... Did Rutgers issue one to every damn idiot with an acceptance letter and a dick?

Grabbing hold of the bar, I steady myself while staring into a pair of bloodshot green eyes.

"Sorry, baby," he slurs. "If you're gonna flash the goods, don't be shocked when someone tries a sample."

I fight to rein in my temper. *If he only knew...* Instead

of smirking, he should be counting his blessings that we're in New Jersey. Twenty-five hundred miles south and every one of those perfect white teeth would be scattered across the floor.

Along with that hand.

And other favored appendages.

Luckily, both our nights are saved when the bartender clears his throat behind me. "Francesca?"

I twist back around. "Huh?"

He flips my ID between his fingers and holds it up between us. "Francesca Romano..." Glancing down at it, he cocks an eyebrow. "From Louisville, Kentucky?"

I cringe. The guy who sold us the fake IDs promised efficacy, not accuracy.

I keep my mouth shut and pay for my drink, deciding to slip the guy an extra twenty just to be safe. By the time I turn back around, the idiot who grabbed my ass is nowhere to be found. Instinctively, I sling an accusing glare to my right, only to find RJ scrolling through his phone, still sitting at the same high-top table he's been brooding over since following me through the door.

I let out a relieved breath. Despite my thoughts to the contrary, I have no desire to be the cause of another man's death.

Glancing up, he catches my eye, his bored expression turning to granite. Although stuffed in a designer suit, his oversized frame looks out of place sitting in the middle of a trendy dance club. He doesn't look like he's here to have a good time. He looks like he's here to shoot up the place.

Which, to be fair, isn't out of the realm of possibility.

RJ's last name may be Harcourt, but he's a Carrera to his

core—and just like Santi, he's deadliest when he's silent.

Don't poke the bear, Lola...

But I can't help myself. I'm hardwired to push boundaries.

Tossing him a salutatory wave, I arch an eyebrow at the phone clutched in his hand and free the snarky smile I've held back since leaving my apartment.

He scowls in response, dropping his phone on the table like it burned him. *That's what I thought. Busted, big guy.* My smile widens, which causes him to fold his arms tightly across his chest and stare at the shot in my hand like it's a glass of battery acid.

Sighing, I leave him and his euthanized sense of humor behind and meander my way through the crowded club. *I miss my cousin.* The one who used to play hide-and-go-seek with me all over the estate. The one who snuck me my first taste of tequila behind the counter of his father's Houston cantina.

The one who used to laugh.

RJ doesn't laugh much anymore. Not since he abandoned his Texas roots and followed Santi to New Jersey two years ago to become his second-in-command and first shield.

The brother and cousin I once knew are gone. They've molded themselves into replicas of their fathers.

Leaving those thoughts behind, I stop a few feet away from the dance floor, my gaze sliding up a private staircase leading to a roped off VIP area. For the second time tonight, the same thought floats through my head.

If they only knew...

If only I didn't have to hide. If only I could flash my last name like an all-access pass, *that's* where I'd be instead of fighting for a drink at a crowded bar.

"María! Over here!"

I glance over my shoulder to find Avery waving frantically from the edge of the dance floor. From the looks of it, she took her own wardrobe advice to heart. That fire-engine red number she's wearing is *almost* a dress.

If it covered her ass.

"All right, María Diaz," I mutter under my breath. "It's showtime."

I don't waste time sipping my shot—I inhale it. Warmth floods my veins, my eyes closing for a beat as thoughts of my stalker invade my head. *As the feel of him still sticks to my skin.*

Not only has he infected my mind, he's branded me... *twice.*

Once without my consent, and once in spite of it.

Opening my eyes again, I stare at the dance floor and at Avery and my friends' smiling faces. With each passing second, my anger escalates.

I envy their blissful ignorance. They're not mice. They're not trapped by a sadistic Santiago just waiting to strike.

That's it.

I slam my empty glass onto the crowded table beside me, ignoring a wave of irritated protests as I stalk toward the dance floor.

How dare Sam violate my apartment and then dismiss me. I'm the daughter of a drug lord. I don't get caught in someone else's head-on collision.

I cause my own.

The base is heavy, and the beat is loud—perfect for drowning out the thoughts poisoning my head. There's no talking. No bullshitting. It's too damn loud to do anything but let the tequila take over.

Before long, everything fades into the background. I just dance, pretending to be normal for a few unguarded moments, until I feel a hard chest press up against me from behind. I stiffen as two rough hands anchor onto my hips, pulling me against something even harder.

Shit. If RJ sees this, we're both screwed.

An automatic reaction has me scanning scan the club, searching for a pair of murderous eyes. Thankfully, the crowd is too thick, allowing me to wiggle out of the guy's hold before the Mexican *sicario* in my cousin erupts and incites a riot.

Twisting around, I extend my arm to put a safe amount of space between us. "No thanks," I yell over the music.

"Why?" he shouts back, those damn hands making a grab for my hips again. "You got a guy or something?"

It doesn't matter if I've "got" a guy, a girl, or a gorilla. If he touches me again, he'll be pulling back a bloody stump.

"No, I—" The minute I look up, the words die on my tongue. On the second level—right in the heart of the VIP area I was just pining over—stands the man I've been waiting for.

Sam is draped over the railing, wearing that irritatingly familiar blasé expression, as if daring it to fall.

A blurry memory breaks through the haze. I remember thinking the same thing last night as I watched him leaning against the wall. How even his stance seemed like a challenge…

"What the hell is he doing here?"

A pair of dry lips dust my ear. "Who?"

I don't bother answering. *Who* isn't the right question. It's *why*.

The longer I stare, the harder Sam stares. *Pinche cabrón.*

Has he been here the whole time? Just watching me like the stalker he is?

He wants a show? For the first time, I offer him a loaded smile. *I'll give him one.*

"Nobody," I shout back. "Let's dance." Before he can grab me again, I shuffle around behind him, causing him to do a one-eighty.

However, my attention isn't on my dance partner. It's one floor up, locked in a battle of wills.

I want a front row seat too, you son of a bitch.

Oblivious, the guy follows my lead and turns to face the VIP area as well. Once again, he hooks an arm around my waist, this time pressing his chest so tightly against my back his shirt sticks to my bare skin. I play the game with cat-like finesse, purring up against him while holding Sam's volatile glare.

The blank expression is gone. His arms are no longer leisurely draped over the railing. Now, he's choking the life out of it.

Instead of deterring me, it spurs me on.

I don't know if it's because I'm taunting him, or if it's because he's jealous—*but screw it.* I'm turning up the heat and pushing the needle to find out once and for all.

Lifting one arm, I coil it around the guy's neck and drop down low, my shiny silver dress riding up my thighs. Slowly and methodically, I rise to the sound of a strained groan behind me.

I know I'm playing another dangerous game, but I've already poured gasoline on a lit flame. All that's left is to watch it burn.

Unfortunately, my attention is forced away from my fiery

creation, when a wandering hand slides up the inside of my thigh.

"Hey!" Spinning around, I shove my fist into his chest. "If you value your testicles, you won't do that again."

The asshole has the nerve to look shocked, muttering, "Tease..." before stalking off the dance floor toward the bar.

"Well, that backfired." I palm the back of my neck just as Avery gives me two thumbs up from a few feet away—like she did last night with Troy.

I'm seriously starting to question the people I've chosen to surround myself with. Their judge of character leaves a lot to be desired.

I grind my teeth together. I'm not exactly a shining beacon of sensibility, myself. I have no idea what this thing is between Sam and me. *And that savage look in his eyes?* I don't know if it's because he wants to hate me or hates that he wants me.

I tell myself not to—but it's useless. My gaze draws back up to the VIP area, only to find the railing empty. He's nowhere to be found.

My heart sinks.

It's neither. He just hates me.

Dejected, I wave my hand to get RJ's attention. Other than pointing toward the ladies' room, then motioning for him to stay put, I don't bother to tell anyone where I'm going as I walk toward the back of the club.

Maybe a few moments of solitude behind a bathroom stall will unfuck my head.

Just as I take my place at the end of a long line, the back door opens, and two girls reenter the club clutching packs of cigarettes and lighters in their hands.

Outside.

That's where I need to go.

Hurrying, I abandon my spot and chase them down a few steps away from the door. "Hi," I say, toning down my accent while pointing at their hands. "Can I bum one of those?"

I have no intention of smoking it. I just need an excuse to be on the other side of that door.

The taller one shrugs and flips the cardboard top open. "Knock yourself out."

Smiling in gratitude, I slide one cigarette from the pack. Before I can even take a step, the same girl lays a heavy hand on my shoulder.

"You plan to light that on someone's tailpipe, honey?" Chuckling, she flicks her thumb on her lighter, presenting me with a dancing flame.

Guess, I'm smoking it now…

I force another smile. "Oh, right. Thank you." Tucking it between my lips, I lean down and suck on the filter, inhaling the disgusting thing until the end burns a bright orange.

Dios mío, I need air.

Throwing all my weight against the door, I tumble out into a dark alleyway and nearly gag. *Air yes—fresh air, not so much.* All I can smell is rancid garbage and this stupid cigarette.

But at least I can finally breathe.

Mostly.

Leaning against the bricks, I take a long drag and sigh. "What the hell is happening to me?"

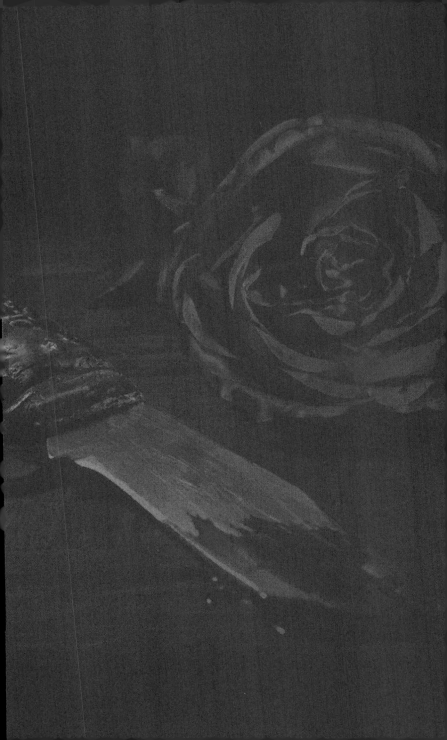

CHAPTER
Eleven

SAM

I can't take my eyes off her dress. It's fucking hypnotic. The way the silver material skims her breasts and hips makes it even more precious than gold to me.

It comes with a warning—a precursor to violence.

So far, there are two victims in this club who didn't read the fine print… The man who pinched her ass as she stood at the bar? *He's on his way to the ER with two broken wrists.* The man who dared to dance with her just now? *He'll soon be lying unconscious in a bathroom stall.*

No hesitation.

No regrets.

After Santiago requested I stay close to Lola, we've been moving in ever-decreasing circles around one another.

Never speaking.

Always watching.

Switching venues from the college campus to this club, my Mexican *dulzura* shining brighter than the sun, as I keep in the shadows.

Tonight, she's the one who's picking up the pace. She's meeting my eyes, returning my hunger, flirting with other men on purpose to tempt me into the spotlight...

All we're doing here is building anticipation for the final scene.

Our crash is inevitable.

"Want another drink, buddy?"

"Bourbon," I tell the bartender, tossing a twenty onto the counter. *I'm in league with the devil these days. I may as well start drinking like him.*

Taking a swig, I watch as Lola leaves the dance floor, her silver dress catching in the club's disco balls—reflecting the kind of sin I want to drown in.

She's moving toward the bathroom stalls, ditching her idiot friends on the dance floor, and murmuring a "stay, boy," at her discreet bodyguard.

Finishing up my drink, I follow ten steps behind, smiling to myself as she ducks out of the line by the ladies' room and heads toward the fire exit at the end of the hallway.

She disappears into the night.

I go to follow when my phone starts chiming. Yanking the device out of my back pocket, I check the ID and accept the call immediately.

"Troublemaking again, Sanders?" comes a familiar clipped drawl.

I bark out a rough laugh. There are few men I'd take orders from, never mind ridicule, but I respect the hell out of

Edier Grayson. I'd even go so far as to call him a friend.

He's five years older than me, but he's not the kind of man who judges age over the ability to fire a gun.

His father is Dante Santiago's second. As such, we grew up together. Stole cars and smoked weed together. *Dared to share our dreams of another life together.*

I stopped running from destiny long before he did.

At eighteen, he was all set to study fine arts at Goldsmiths in London. Then he switched from a kid to a killer overnight. Trading pencils for bullets, he's spent the last couple of years in South America slaughtering the last of Santiago's enemies and shoring up the distribution channels from Cartagena until a recent move to the East Coast brought his talents to the US.

He's cool as fuck...

With a sting like a scorpion.

And if the tone of his voice is anything to go by? *He's pissed as hell.*

"Where are you?"

"New Brunswick."

He blows out a breath. "I want you back in NYC within the hour. I need a closure and then a clean-up. You good for that?"

It's another test. One that requires a gun, two fists, and an absence of morality.

Check, check, and double check. The more I integrate myself in the organization, the more sway I'll have over Lola Carrera's fate.

"I'll be there in fifty," I tell him as silver swims with crimson. "Message me the address."

Hanging up, I slip into the alley. She's standing a couple

of feet away in the moonlight with her back turned. *Braced.* A perfect silhouette that's mine for the taking.

As I watch, she tips her head back and exhales, her long dark hair tumbling to her waist as tendrils of smoke coil around her like a dirty halo. She's smoking to justify why she's out here, but the time for pretense is over.

We both know what she's waiting for.

Me.

This.

When she hears the soft click of the door closing behind me, her shoulders stiffen. The lit cigarette drops from her fingers, flaring orange as it hits the asphalt by her heels.

I move fast. Before she has a chance to speak, my hand is clamped across her mouth, and I'm spinning her face-first into the wall.

"Have you come here to play, little mouse?" I murmur as the sweet scent from her apartment is amplified a thousand times.

It's all around me.

Consuming me.

Eliciting the filthiest thoughts.

I think of my cum smearing her mirror and basin.

I think of my cum dripping from her lips.

She moans her response into my hand. She tries to fight me off, bucking her hips and twisting. *Not that I'd expect anything less...*

I press her body even harder into the wall, crushing my own knuckles in the process and drawing blood. Her flighty breaths are music to my ears. I need to return to New York, but first, I'll leave my Mexican *dulzura* with a dirty narrative to replay in my absence.

Keeping one hand on her mouth, I trail my fingers up the damp heat of her inner thighs. She shudders and stops fighting the minute I reach her panties.

Wet.

Soaking.

I couldn't stay away from her if I tried.

"Is this for me, Lola?" I say huskily, resisting the urge to slide her panties to the side and sink my middle finger inside her. "Such a gift from my angel in black, *and silver*. Because that's what you are...*the fucking death of me*."

She moans again, squirming helplessly against my touch.

"I hate you, too," I say with a low chuckle. "You know, I'd fuck you right here in this alley if I thought it would loosen these chains between us." I lean in closer. Citrus... *My heaven and my hell*. "Turns out, they're unbreakable, but I think you know that already."

Glancing down, I bite out a groan when I see how flawlessly we fit together.

Her ass.

My dick.

Her pussy.

My fingers.

I won't be satisfied until every part of her is submitting to me. *Demanding me.*

Maybe it's time to leave a different kind of memory on her body—a reminder of just how brutal and beautiful our connection is.

Dropping my hand from her pussy, I reach for the gun tucked into the back waistband of my Levis and commence a new path up the inside of her thighs, swapping warm skin for cold steel.

Moans turn to muffled screams.

"You keep me in a prison cell for you, Lola," I accuse, kicking her legs apart. "With rusty bars on the windows and a broken lock. As punishment, I'm going to blur the lines between fear and lust. The first time you come for me will be from the sweetest act of violence."

Muffled screams turn to whimpers, as I drag the muzzle across her clit.

I do it again, and again, rubbing out a rhythm that has her whimpering, and me throbbing against the zipper of my jeans, leaking pre-cum.

My lips twitch as she slams her palms against the wall and widens her legs even more for me. It's a full-blown smile when she starts grinding up and down the barrel of my gun, seeking relief from something that's just as filthy as I am.

I press harder.

I rub faster.

My mind briefly wanders back a few hours ago in her bathroom, when I was just as unforgiving with myself.

I finger the trigger to flood the moment with even more danger. She shudders, but doesn't stop. *She can't stop.* We're not just crossing lines anymore. We're fucking obliterating them. Normal doesn't exist for us. When you're born into the threat of violence, it warps everything.

Dropping my hand from her mouth, I force my fingers between her teeth, needing to feel the strength of her orgasm as strands of black silk whip across my face—nearly coming myself as she bites down hard with another scream, piercing the skin.

Afterward, we collapse forward, both breathing hard.

"Soon," I gasp, removing my gun from between her thighs. Despising it. Envying it. "Soon, every part of you will be mine, Lola."

"Soon," she whispers in concession, one cheek pressed tightly against the brickwork—as twisted up by this as I am.

Not that I'm giving her a choice, either way.

She stays motionless where she is as I slide back into the shadows, thinking how stunning she looks all destroyed like this.

She waits until she thinks I've gone, but I'll never leave her alone while she's vulnerable. Instead, I watch unseen as she peels herself away from the wall. Her steps are unsteady as she heads toward the door.

Mission accomplished.

She won't be thinking about anything else now until the next time we meet.

And there will always be a next time with her.

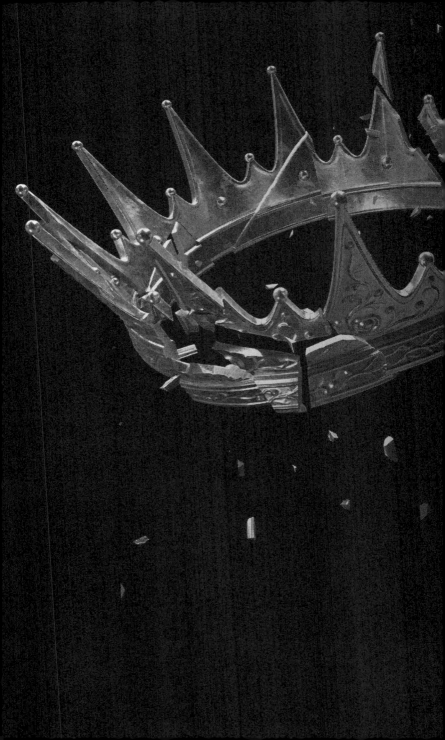

CHAPTER
Twelve

LOLA

My mother has a saying…
Chasing butterflies only leads you into repetitive circles. Pretend they don't exist, and they'll flutter back into the palm of your hand.

At ten years old, I took those words at face value. I spent hours sitting cross-legged on the bright green lawns of our estate, my arms spread wide and my palms up.

Waiting.

A butterfly never landed in my hand. They always darted around me, close enough to admire, but just out of reach.

I realize now—as most things with my family—it was a metaphorical warning. Butterflies are just like boys. Chase them, and they fly away. Leave them be, and they come to you.

A valuable lesson I wish I'd remembered days ago. *Four to be exact.*

A full ninety-six hours since I've seen or heard from Sam.

After our alleyway encounter, he just disappeared—as if successfully breaking me meant there was no more game left to play.

He'd won. I'd lost. End of story.

Only it wasn't—at least for me.

I always have the last word, but he left me speechless while he rode away like some kind of dark knight. So, instead of pretending he didn't exist, I chased a butterfly.

I've become the stalker.

For four days, I've driven by his apartment at all hours of the night just to catch a glimpse of him. I've casually inquired on his whereabouts around campus. Worst of all...? I've stood in the alleyway outside the Foxhole, shamelessly waiting for him to reappear.

I've spun in so many circles, I've made myself dizzy.

So after receiving nothing but silence, I decided it was time to put Eden Lachey Carrera's motherly advice to the test.

That's how I ended up here, at a dive college bar, sharing a plate of nachos with some frat boy I don't even like.

I suppose Alex-*what's-his-name* is nice enough—*cheap as hell*—but nice. However, I'm not interested. Not even those All-American dimples can divert my attention away from the man who owns my thoughts.

I used to crave normalcy—a clichéd, bland existence. Thanks to Sam and his filthy brand of debauchery, I now crave rebellion. I hunger to push boundaries and test my own limits. I wait for the sun to go down so I can dance in the darkness.

His darkness.

Sighing, I toss a half-eaten tortilla chip onto my plate and pull a fresh water bottle from my purse. Unscrewing the cap, I drink slowly so I don't have to engage in pointless small talk.

"You know they have water here, right?"

Resting the rim of the bottle against my bottom lip, I give him a half-hearted smile. "I have a rule against drinking things that aren't sealed these days." At his furrowed brow, I add, "A girl can never be too careful."

But she can definitely be too desperate—something I hope to rectify tonight.

There's an awkward silence as Alex spins his phone in lazy circles on the table. "So, what's your major?"

It's all I can do not to roll my eyes. This is what this sick obsession of mine has come to—engaging in useless chatter with a cardboard placeholder.

"Don't have one yet," I say, sliding out of the sticky booth. "I'm only a few weeks into my freshman year." Before he can offer up another mundane question, I hold up one finger while already walking away. "Be right back. Have to use the ladies' room."

Of course, I'm headed nowhere near the ladies' room... *Again.*

Weaving my way around scratched tables and barstools, I disappear down a secluded hallway toward what I hope is the back door.

One that leads to another darkened alley, maybe...?

Nostalgia is a ruthless bitch.

But before I can take another step, a firm hand is wrapping around my arm and dragging me into an alcove.

"Where the hell do you think you're going?"

Gritting my teeth, I tug my arm out of RJ's claw-like grip

and spin around ready to spit fire. "Outside."

"Don't think so."

If I have to deal with one more male ego…

"Don't you have something better to do than babysit me?"

Wrong thing to say, Lola.

Even bathed in shadow, I see the hard clench of his jaw and the warning in those onyx eyes. "Yeah, I do—like run this goddamn East Coast operation for your brother. Unfortunately, little *chaparrita* decided to swim with the sharks and got herself bit."

I recoil at the sharp accusation. RJ Harcourt is as efficient as they come. He doesn't believe in wasting time or resources doing mundane tasks or…

Chasing butterflies.

I cross my arms over my chest. "That's not fair."

"Life isn't fair, Lola. If it was…" His voice trails off, leaving the rest unspoken.

Left to ambiguous interpretation.

Only, he forgets how well I know him. How I see through that iron façade of his, right down to his hidden truth.

If it was, Santi would be here with you while I called the shots, I think, silently finishing his bold presumption for myself.

I know he's loyal to my brother, but there has always been an unspoken, underlying rivalry between them. RJ is a year older, and after a childhood filled with death and loss, he's much more streetwise. Whereas Santi boasts birthright and stealth, RJ operates on survival and brawn.

They're a dormant volcano just waiting for the right storm. Carrera men crave power, not servitude. I worry what will happen when they inevitably clash.

Speaking of volcanoes...

"Shouldn't you be on a date of your own?" I ask with a conspiratorial smile.

"What the fuck is that supposed to mean?"

Heaving out an exasperated sigh, I slump against the wall. "Don't try and play innocent with me, RJ. I'm better at it than you." I should probably drop and refrain from waving any more red flags, but I don't. "You know exactly what, or should I say *who* I'm talking about. Long, curly, brown hair? Legs like a ballerina? Two boulders on her chest the size of—"

He clamps his hand over my mouth. "That's enough."

I smile against his palm, remembering his obsession with his phone the other night and knowing who was most likely on the other line. *The same woman I've seen him tucked in dark corners with for weeks now.*

"Who is she?" I mumble into his palm.

"Nobody."

I cock an eyebrow, my words still muffled as I counter, "Didn't look like *nobody* to me."

He presses harder, flattening my lips. "You know nothing, Lola. You got me?"

In response, I stare down at the hand still smooshing my face and wait. Letting out a rough growl, he draws back and shoves it in his pocket.

"Yeah," I tell him, elated not to be the only one in this family with secrets. "I got you. What Santi doesn't know won't hurt him. *You got me?*"

RJ grunts out a reluctant affirmation.

"Good." I nod. "Now that that's settled, how about you

head back to Newark?"

"And do what?"

"Tell my brother I left my date early, and I'm now safe and sound and *alone* in my apartment."

It's his turn to cock an eyebrow. "And you think he's gonna buy that bullshit?"

"If you're the one shoveling it? Yes."

I can all but hear the scales tipping back and forth in his head. It's a gamble—one that requires a lot of trust and faith. Two unfamiliar words when it comes to Carrera men.

Finally, RJ exhales on a harsh breath. "You'll go straight home after this?"

Right. Despite what he wants me to think he's agreeing to, we both know he'll be following me home anyway. The man is secretive, not suicidal.

However, just like a few nights ago at the club, I give him a mock salute. "Scout's honor."

He shakes his head. "You're trouble, Carrera."

"Takes one to know one, Harcourt."

Raking one hand over the top of his closely-cropped dark hair, he ruffles mine with the other. "One of these days, you're gonna go looking for it in the wrong place, and instead of causing trouble, you're gonna fall neck deep in the middle of it."

"Duly noted," I say, giving him a small smile. I have no interest in pressing my luck, so with a quick pat to his chest, I speed walk back to the table.

Alex glances up, his forehead wrinkling as I slide back into the booth. "Everything okay?"

"Fine," I counter, waving a dismissive hand, as if I haven't been missing for over fifteen minutes. "Long line. You know how it is."

By the look on his face, he doesn't, but then again, neither do I. I'm just trying to keep him from asking questions he doesn't want the answers to.

"So, María, what do you say we—?"

"I'm really tired," I blurt out, padding the statement with an exaggerated yawn. "Do you mind taking me home?"

"We've been here less than half an hour."

I offer a lukewarm smile. *Yeah, and my chances of catching a butterfly is slim to none at this point.* It seems my mother's sage advice doesn't apply to a certain rebel without a conscience.

I'd be wasting both of our time if I pretended otherwise.

"I'm sorry. I have a really bad headache all of a sudden." I tilt my head, trying to appear apologetic. "Raincheck?"

He's not happy as he snatches a twenty-dollar bill from his wallet and then slams it face down onto the table.

That makes two of us.

Something aches all right, but it's definitely not my head.

———

This was a huge mistake.

I'm barely present as Alex pulls his blue Prius into the parking lot outside my apartment building. I should've never agreed to this date.

I should've learned my lesson about stepping outside the lines a week ago.

"Thanks. I really appreciate—" My words are cut off by a

pair of demanding lips.

My palms shoot forward against his chest, but just before I push him away, a taunting voice whispers inside my head... *Don't chase butterflies—provoke them.*

So, dancing on a very thin tightrope, I do the unthinkable.

I let it happen.

Alex-*what's-his-name's* kiss is wet and uninspiring, a pathetic substitute for the forbidden one I can't stop craving. The cruel touch of a man and his gun—both of which I dreamed about last night in such vivid detail, I woke up blushing from the sheer depravity of it.

Nothing like the fumbling, hurried hand attempting to unbutton my dress.

No. This is all wrong.

"Stop!" Shoving him away, I tumble into the passenger's seat, wiping the remnants of his sloppy kiss away with the back of my hand.

"Come on, baby," he urges, diving his hand into my hair and twisting the strands around his fingers. "Don't play hard to get."

Damn, that hurts.

"I'm not trying to." Wincing, I pull away, only to get yanked back across the console. "But I also don't put out on the first date."

Or at all...

"That's not what I heard."

I glare up at him, his smug accusation as cold as my brother's soul. "What the hell did you hear?"

My date leans in, his breath hot on my cheek. "Everybody's saying you fucked Troy Davis at Sam Colton's party."

Emotion clouds my judgment, and I don't think; I swing, a damn impressive right hook catching him across the chin.

"Son of a bitch!" he yells, releasing my hair to cover his face. "What the fuck?"

Holy shit, I have no idea what the hell just happened. It's as if the brand on my hip has infected my blood with venom. I'm drunk with power and feeding off the poison coursing through my veins.

Maybe I'm not as innocent as everyone thinks.

"I'm getting out now." I smile sweetly, the glassy confusion in his eyes fueling my sadistic enjoyment. "And if I hear a word around campus that anything happened between you and me other than a kiss goodnight, your football career will be over faster than Troy's." *And if Troy's unfortunate warehouse destination is any indication, his life as well.* "Are we clear?"

Alex's face blanches. "Get out of my car, you crazy bitch."

Opening the passenger's side door, I blow him a kiss and make my way toward my apartment, a strange smile on my face.

Maybe I didn't catch a butterfly tonight, but I caught the scent of something way more potent.

My own darkness.

CHAPTER
Thirteen

SAM

Edier is watching me closely again.

He's had me locked in a cage of scrutiny ever since I returned to New York. He knows I'm distracted, but he's choosing his moment to question me about it.

He's so much like his father in that respect. Patience is a virtue in the Grayson family. The Senator once told me how he'd tortured a man for five days before he finally broke him. Slow and steady... An extracted tooth here. A slipped confession there.

Edier has been taking notes.

"Finish him," he orders, turning away from the bruised and bloodied man hanging by his wrists from the meat hook—suspended between life and death.

I take out my gun and pull the trigger, making the Russian my fourth kill in as many days. Murdering the last of my boyhood along with Savio the snitch.

People try to take advantage during a power change. It's like they think the incoming king has cracks of stupidity in his crown. The moment Edier stepped foot in New York, the Russians started flexing their muscles. A couple of trusted Santiago dealers ended up with their throats slit, so retribution was demanded.

After this week, no one will be questioning Edier's authority in this town again.

Twenty-six dead.

A Bratva cell in flames.

Even the Italians down on Canal Street have stopped strutting their shit like peacocks on a day outing.

It scares me how easily I've slipped into this new life. It's like a designer suit with bloodstains that's been tailored just for me.

I find Edier waiting outside the meat warehouse.

"Tell Reece to get rid of the bodies." His face is still as fuck, no flickers of emotion, but you know what they say about those kinds of waters... "You did well."

"Do I get a glitter sticker and a lollipop?"

Edier stares at me for a beat before his lips start twitching. "There he is.... Sam the sarcastic pain-in-the-ass. I was beginning to think you'd undergone a personality transplant at that fancy college of yours."

"Ex-college," I correct, as he folds a piece of gum into his mouth and pockets the wrapper. He chews slowly. Methodically. A twenty-five-year-old cartel prince with the habits of a high school chick.

"You're playing with fire."

"Nice day to get burned."

His eyebrows lift at my tone. "Seems the joker grew teeth."

"I'm not handing her over to Santiago," I warn.

"Who says you have a choice?"

Cursing under my breath, I start walking toward my Bugatti. I've been gone for too long. I have a tracking device on her car. I've hacked the college and her apartment security cameras. I know the moment she wakes up and the hour she falls asleep, but it's still not enough.

I can feel the weight of my gun pressing against my heart. *The same gun that made such a pretty mess of that composure.*

I start the engine as Edier taps on the window.

"Screw her out of your system, and then I want you back in New York by Friday," he says tersely. "She's a Carrera, Sam... I don't need to spell out all the bullshit that comes with that name."

I jerk out a nod, tearing at my lower lip in frustration. *And obsessions don't just "leave your system," Edier. They dig deep with spikes until nothing shakes them lose. They puncture your lungs so you need their fucking air to survive.*

Something flashes in his dark eyes. Something close to sympathy.

"Listen, Ella Santiago arrives here next week for a late transfer into NYU, and I want you supervising her protection. If anything happens to the devil's daughter on my watch, I'll end up on a meat hook next to Savio. You hear me?"

I jerk out another nod.

"Go." Taking a step back from the car, he slides his hands into his pockets. "And don't come back until you're breathing Santiago fumes again, not Carrera's."

———————

I boomerang straight back to New Brunswick, braking with a screech outside her apartment—parking at an angle and blocking off two spaces.

I checked the trackers on the way here, my mood souring somewhere along the Garden State Freeway. Her place is in darkness, but I know exactly where she is, and she knows she'll be getting punished for it.

Taking the fire exit stairs, I do what I need to do, and then I'm swinging back into my Bugatti to move it to a more discreet location around the side of the building.

Just as well.

A minute later, Santi Carrera pulls up and stalks inside, leaving three of his men by the door.

Soon after, a blue Ford Prius is parking nearby.

I watch the scene play out in grim silence, knowing I can't make a goddamn move with her brother and his *sicarios* in the vicinity. Instead, I satisfy myself with the fact I'll be adding a fifth kill to my lack of conscience by the end of the night.

I'm starting to forget who I was before Lola. Did I crack jokes like Edier said I did? *Act more carefree?*

As soon as she exits the car, I'm ramming a fresh magazine into my Glock. Ten minutes later, I'm rear-ending a blue Ford Prius off the road and watching some college prick piss himself with fear.

When I return to her apartment, I'm still buzzing with unrestrained violence, bloody knuckles, and a Lola-shaped hole in my heart that only she can fill.

CHAPTER
Fourteen

LOLA

It's well after midnight, and the blackness blanketing the sky matches the one filling my apartment as I walk inside. As expected, just as we pulled into the parking lot, RJ's headlights followed behind us.

Apparently, we both like playing with fire.

Now, not only do I have my designated babysitter back on duty, it seems the powers-that-be have called in reinforcements.

Three to be exact.

A fortified wall of emotionless *sicarios* who don't give a damn what I want or think.

Super.

Although I can't see anything, my confidence is in control and leading the charge, while common sense lounges somewhere three or four rungs down the ladder.

Another of my father's warnings filters through my head as I cross the threshold into the living room. *Arrogance can be your strongest asset or your weakest flaw.*

Arrogance is why I don't bother turning on the lights.

Or maybe the mouse just wants to be caught.

"You're late."

I stumble into the wall, letting out something between a gasp and a shriek, when the lamp beside the couch clicks on. Harsh yellow light spills across the room, illuminating the man sitting on my couch. His favored slicked-back dark hair is wild and chaotic, casting a stark contrast against the pristine white leather and giving him a sinister glow. Three buttons on his shirt are open at the collar, highlighting the strained muscles in his neck that lead to one hell of a pissed-off scowl.

Adrenaline deflates from my chest, and I sigh in both relief and irritation. "¡*Ay Dios mío*, Santi! What the hell?"

"Pack your shit," he deadpans, his expression tight.

"Excuse me?"

"Did I stutter?" Rising to his feet, my brother crosses the room, all six foot four inches of him looming over me like a warden. "You're leaving for Mexico tonight."

I stare up at him, blinking rapidly as if the movement will force clarity into those five words. "What?"

"You heard what I said."

"I have a life here!" I shout, my panic escalating as I move in front of him, blocking his path. "My *own* life with my *own* friends. I don't want to leave it."

"I didn't ask what you wanted, *chaparrita*. You're leaving, and that's final."

Final. He growls the word like *papá*. As if his command

is the damn gospel. As if I'm not an adult with a brain and free will. *Granted, an adult who disobeyed him and got herself roofied and branded, but that's beside the point...*

I fling my arms around like a broken windmill. "Do I not get a say in this?"

"No."

I want him to yell. Instead, he remains rigid and stoic. "Santi!"

"This is not up for discussion." He steps forward, and I automatically step back. "I warned you to stay away from Sanders, and you wouldn't listen. Now they know."

"Know *what*?" I demand. "And who's *they*?" He's talking in circles, and I'm tired of standing on the outside of them while trying to decipher Carrera cryptic talk.

"Dante Santiago," he bites out between clenched teeth. "My contacts in New York saw him pay Senator Sanders a visit a few days ago. Care to guess the main topic of conversation?"

My stomach plummets to my feet. "Me?"

He doesn't confirm nor deny. Instead, he paces in front of me, another trait he inherited from our father. The more he paces, the faster he talks. "Your cover is blown, *chaparrita*. They know María Diaz is an alias. They know who you are, and now they're going to use you to get to me and *papá*. We can't take that chance, so you're going back to Mexico where the cartel can protect you."

I can't stop staring at the dark circles flashing under his eyes every time he passes me. Jesus, it looks like he hasn't slept in days...maybe weeks. I noticed it at the pizzeria, but it's gotten worse. His obsession with this feud between our family and the Santiagos is consuming him.

"There's nothing I can do to change your mind?"

"No." When he faces me, I recoil, the brother I grew up with disappearing behind the hardened mask of a criminal. "You're in over your head, Lola. You're drowning, and you don't even know it."

A surge of fury courses through me, prompting me to hurl my purse against the wall. "Damn it, Santi! I'm eighteen, not eight! You can't force me to leave the country. I'm just as much of a Carrera as you are. For Christ's sake, I just punched a guy in the face for trying to get into my pants."

Which was absolutely the wrong thing to say.

Santi's dark eyebrows shoot up to his messy hairline. "You *what*?"

"Focus, please," I huff, redirecting the conversation. "The point is that you can't keep ordering me around like this. You're my brother, not my father."

He gets deathly quiet. The strained kind of quiet where you know you've fucked up. The kind that fills the air with so much static it crackles. "You're right," he says calmly. "I'm not." His jaw tics as he reaches into his pocket and pulls out his phone. Without a word, he presses a single button.

"What are you doing?" I whisper.

His narrowed eyes snap to mine. "Proving a point."

Within seconds, he's speaking into the phone in rapid Spanish. It's my native language, so, of course, I understand every word, yet somehow it all gets muddled in my brain, hovering in that space between willful ignorance and denied truth.

Before the fog in my head can clear, he presses another

button and holds the phone between us.

"*Cielito*," a deep, heavily accented voice rumbles.

Oh fuck.

"*Papá?*" I have no idea why his name exits my mouth as a question. There's no mistaking Valentin Carrera's voice. I've witnessed grown men piss themselves at the mere sound of it.

"We had a deal, *cielito*."

"I know, *papá*, but—"

"No buts," he clips, cutting off my protest. "Your *mamá* and I allowed you to attend school under the direct supervision and discretion of your brother. Santi has informed me that your alias and safety have been compromised."

I glare at my brother. *Snitch.* "But, *papá*…"

"*¡Silencio!*"

I jump at the harsh command in his tone. My father has never raised his hand to me, but that doesn't mean he isn't terrifying. I may be *papá's* little girl, but even *I* know when to shut the hell up.

"I almost lost you once at the hands of Dante Santiago," he continues. "I will not risk my daughter's life again. Your brother and I have many enemies, *cielito*. Enemies who would love nothing more than to see you suffer for our sins. So, you *will* pack your shit, and you *will* board my jet with RJ and return to Mexico City immediately."

Oh great, a traveling companion.

I don't know what possesses me to ask, "And if I don't?"

Dumb, Lola. Dumb, dumb, dumb.

Even Santi lifts an eyebrow.

"Lola…" It's a grave warning. My father only uses my given name when I'm about to fall out of his good graces. It's a dark place no one wants to find themselves, whether family, friend, or foe.

I swallow hard. "*Sí, papá.*"

"Santi," he growls. "Take me off speaker phone."

Obeying, my brother disappears into the kitchen to discuss cartel business with our father in an unnecessarily hushed tone. He could act out their entire battle strategy in an interpretive dance for all I care. I'm not interested in anything they have to say. I'm too devastated at the blow I've just been dealt.

My taste of freedom.

My chance at a normal life.

All gone because of a stupid obsession.

I wander around my apartment, soaking in the last moments of normalcy I have left. Sighing, I trail my hand over the white leather couch Santi cursed to hell for over an hour as he carried it up two flights of stairs. I dust my finger along the top of the flat screen TV, still hanging crooked on the wall after RJ refused to use a leveler.

All snapshots of independence soon to be a distant memory.

Stopping next to the window, I move the curtain to gaze out at the empty parking lot, when a flash of color catches my eye, causing my stomach to somersault.

A yellow Post-it Note is stuck to the glass. With a shaking hand, I tear it away and read the familiar slanted handwriting.

When the mouse strays, she gets punished. Slowly, painfully, until she begs for mercy. This time, it won't be steel that draws it from her. The hunt is on, dulzura.

CHAPTER
Fifteen

LOLA

The pulse in my neck beats a furious rhythm. *It's him.*
He was here, inside my apartment again.

But how? When?

When the mouse strays, she gets punished.

Lifting my head off the glass, I stare out the window. One that gives a perfect view of the parking lot. *Right where Alex's car was parked.*

I fist my hands, the note crumpling in my damp palm as I stumble backward.

He saw us.

Common sense tells me to feel violated again. Instead, my cheeks heat with desire.

It's exactly what you wanted...

Thoughts swirl in my head of Sam standing where I am now, watching Alex kiss me. Watching him try to undress me.

Watching as I fought back, the Carrera in me surfacing like an uncaged animal.

Did it infuriate him?

Did his dick harden as he watched?

Images spin through my mind faster than I can control them. It's sick and twisted, but I can't stop. The more I think about him—his jaw tight, his need strong, and his hate for me, a barrel of gasoline with my taunting a lit match—the wetter I get.

I can't breathe.

"Lola?"

I jump as my brother's voice rumbles behind me.

"Shit!" Quickly shoving the note into my bra, I turn around, trying to mask arousal as annoyance. "Stop sneaking up on me like that!" As soon as my heart starts beating again, I shift a nervous glance back at the window. "How long had you been here before I walked in?"

"A few minutes. Why?"

No reason. Just wondering if you crossed paths with my stalker. "Never mind."

With as much dignity as possible, I walk past him toward the bedroom, when he grabs my arm.

"What the hell, Santi? Do you or do you not want me to pack?"

He holds out his hand. "Give me your keys."

"You're kidding me, right?"

"Do I look like I'm kidding?"

No, he looks like he's about to throw me over his shoulder and carry me back to Mexico.

There's no hope in changing his mind. I've been a part of

this family long enough to know a losing battle when I see one.

Sighing, I gesture toward the far wall where the contents of my purse lay scattered across the floor. "Help yourself."

Rolling his eyes, he crosses the room and bends down to sift through the strewn contents. After pocketing my keys, he runs a hand through his unruly hair. "I have to make arrangements with RJ. I'll be back in half an hour. Be ready."

Once again, I heave out a heavy sigh.

Santi tips my chin with his forefinger, the hard lines in his face softening. "*Chaparrita*, I'm not doing this to punish you."

"It doesn't feel like it."

"You're my baby sister, Lola. My responsibility. I couldn't live with myself if anything happened to you." His hold tightens. "You have to understand that family is everything to me. I'll kill for you. I'll die for you. And any man who hurts you will suffer until his last breath."

Damn it. His fierce loyalty is making it hard to hate him right now. "I know."

And therein lies the problem. *I do know.* His words aren't just idle threats. He won't rest until Sam pays. Not only for crossing territory lines, but for drawing Carrera blood.

For daring to taint the innocence of Valentin Carrera's daughter.

The gold flecks in Santi's brown eyes glitter with affection. "I love you, kid."

"I love you too," I mumble. *It'd be so much easier if I didn't.*

With a brotherly kiss to my forehead, he leaves me alone with my wayward thoughts and a ticking time clock. Closing the door behind him, I turn and slump against it.

Half an hour.

Half an hour and then it's goodbye freedom, hello shackles and chains. I love my family with all my heart, but they're slowly suffocating me.

"You're in over your head, Lola. You're drowning, and you don't even know it."

How the hell am I supposed to learn to swim if I'm never allowed to sink?

But you did sink, a voice in my head whispers. You sank hard, just like the enemy's blade did into your skin. You moaned for him. You chased the ruthless path of a loaded gun as he dragged it against you. He did more than slice your skin—he sliced through your last shred of restraint.

Biting my lip, I reach into my bra and pull out the Post-it Note. Smoothing out the wrinkles, I read the words again, memorizing each slanted line as I wander back across the living room.

When the mouse strays, she gets punished. Slowly, painfully, until she begs for mercy. This time, it won't be steel that draws it from her. The hunt is on, dulzura.

The hunt is on.

What does that even mean? Is he watching me right now?

Before I can stop myself, I wander back to the window. Scraping my teeth over my bottom lip, I lean against the wooden frame and scour the parking lot.

He's a Santiago associate—my family's sworn enemy. I'm meant to hate him and everything he stands for. According to Santi and *papá*, he wants nothing more than to hurt me.

To kill me.

So, why simply mark me? Why use his gun in that alley

instead of his cock? He's had every chance to taint Valentin Carrera's daughter. To take my virginity and leave me bleeding until I gasped my last breath.

So why didn't he?

I stared across the room into those intense, dark eyes the night of his party, and then again in the nightclub. They weren't drenched in hate. If anything, they radiated lust.

And something else...

Something more unsettling.

Obsession.

I know because it courses through my own veins, too.

I think of his cool demeanor and that midnight black hair, wild and a little long—as reckless and chaotic as the man himself.

He's a silent predator, stalking with beauty and grace and then devouring with the appetite of an entire pack. *Just like he did in the alley when he blurred the line between desire and death.*

He saved me that night from Troy Davis. I can't remember it or prove it, but I know in my soul he did.

As if pulled by a magnetic force, my fingers trail down my dress, between my breasts, down my stomach, and hover just inside of my hip. I touch the still tender S with the tip of my finger. Over and over, I trace the brand he gave me, each pass hardening my nipples to stiff peaks.

I wonder if he's outside this window watching me right now?

"What game are you playing, Sam?" I muse, imagining him standing in the parking lot and looking up at me through the window.

When the mouse strays, she gets punished.

Maybe in another lifetime, yes, but in half an hour, I'll be on a plane to Mexico. Our cat and mouse game is over. There will be no punishment. No begging. No hunt.

No more butterflies to catch.

I'll never see him again, and he'll never see me again.

Unless I let him see me now.

I don't know what possesses me to unbutton the first button at the top of my dress, but the moment I do, a rush of heat pools between my legs so unbearably strong, I can't control myself. I unbutton another…then another…then another…until the entire thing is barely hanging onto my shoulders. I can't see anything outside the window. It's too dark, but I feel him. He's out there watching…*waiting*.

What I'm doing is dangerous. RJ could have left with Santi, or he could be standing guard right outside cataloging my every move. I don't see him lurking about, but that's hardly comforting. Cousin or not, as my brother's right-hand man, he wouldn't hesitate to throw me under the bus.

Electricity sizzles down my spine at the contradiction. Two dark knights—one here to protect my purity, the other here to destroy it.

This is what being a Carrera means. Daring to walk into fire. Balancing on the thin wires tracing my name. Risking the fall just to satiate an innate need to shatter society's perfect ideals.

If I'm going to be convicted, I might as well commit the crime.

My fingers travel up my arm and curl around the strap resting on my shoulder. I'm lightheaded as it slides down my skin, ashamed of my own wantonness, but too far gone to stop. Trailing my hand across my chest, I reach for the strap clinging to my other shoulder, when a faint ringing sound catches my attention.

Turning, I stare across the room at the cell phone lying face down on the floor by my purse, and my stomach clenches.

I don't have to look to know it's RJ. There's no doubt in my mind he's caught an unintentional glimpse of Sam's private show, and he's calling to warn me of my brother's impending wrath.

My heavy footsteps carry me across the room, where I pick up my phone, my indiscretion searing the metal into my palm. The screen is blank, save two words.

Unknown Caller.

Of course. My family uses burner phones. Always helpful when avoiding the DEA. Sighing, I hit the accept button. "RJ, come on... I thought we had a deal? I'm already in enough trouble. Can we just keep this between—?"

A rough breath hisses through the line, licking my ear with its forbidden tongue.

"RJ?"

He doesn't answer, but the breathing grows heavier... lethal...more insistent. There's an underlying growl hidden in the silence that ignites my skin.

It's him.

I don't know how I know; I just do.

Closing my eyes, I imagine his gaze following my every move as that wicked tongue licks his full lips.

"Can you see me, Sam?" I whisper. "Do you want to see your creation?"

Wandering back to the window, I stare into the pitch-black night. Once I verify my cousin is nowhere to be found, my restraint snaps. Emboldened by lust, I push the remaining strap of my dress off my shoulder, not flinching as the material slips past my waist and pools at my feet.

I'm standing in front of my second-floor window in a lacy black bra and thong, breathing as heavily as if he were standing behind me, his lips brushing my neck.

Slowly, I run my fingers along the S puckering the skin on my hip, a strange pride filling my chest. "What does this mean?" I ask, placing a hand against the glass. "Am I marked for death? Or am I marked for *you*?"

As if in response, a bright orange glow ignites in the hazy dark, and then just as quickly, disappears. Startled, I take a few steps back, logic trying to force its way through whatever spell I'm under.

However, instead of getting dressed as any sane person would do, I lick my lips. "Sam…?" I call out, testing him by slowly dragging a bra strap down my shoulder. "Do you like what you see? Is this what you thought about when you got yourself off in my bathroom? Do you want me, or do you just like to watch?"

The image in my head returns, bringing with it an insatiable ache between my thighs. As if commanded, I slide my other strap down, teasing a nipple through the thin lace of my bra. "Did you see me with Alex tonight? What would you have done if I'd let him touch me?" I'm growing delirious with lust, my pussy throbbing at the thought of my father's enemy watching me… Hearing me… "Would you have stopped me? Would you have killed him for it? Do you want to punish me,

Sam?"

Fuck, I can't take it anymore. I slip my hand into my panties, gasping as my finger finds my clit.

"What if I'd let him fuck me?" I groan, rubbing furious circles. The pleasure is so intense it lifts me onto my toes, forcing me to bow my head. "What would you have done?"

In my mind, it's no longer my finger torturing my clit. *It's his.* Stars burst behind my closed eyes as the fantasy pushes me closer to the edge.

"I'm a virgin, you know. Does that get you off?" *Shit!* The glass fogs as I sink my finger inside my wet heat, pumping just like I know he would do. "I'm leaving, Sam." My body is shaking with need, words tumbling out of my mouth with reckless abandon. "Your mouse is being taken away. You could've been my first. Now another will take what's yours. Does that piss you off?"

Letting out a tortured cry, I return to my clit, chasing an orgasm carved in his image.

Pretending my hand is his mouth...his tongue...

"Would you take me hard? Over and over until I bled your name? Until there wasn't a part of me that didn't belong to you?" *That's it.* The thought of him claiming and dominating me is too much. "Sam!" Collapsing against the window, I come violently, his name a hoarse cry on my lips.

When the euphoria of my orgasm finally fades, I slump against the window, my forehead and breasts pressed against the glass, and my hand still tucked inside my panties.

What's even more pathetic?

The fantasy will never be enough.

Quickly ending the call, I block the unknown number in

a panic and push away from the window, staring blankly at my reflection—at my half-naked body and the crude S carved into the inside of my hip.

"You're in over your head, Lola. You're drowning, and you don't even know it."

My brother is right. I'm drowning. I'm getting myself off in front of a window to the thought of my family's sworn enemy, for Christ's sake. The man who desecrated my body in the name of war, not desire.

"That is a metal slab at the medical examiner's office... And that, dear sister, is the same scarlet letter carved into her chest." Santi's warning blares like a siren in my head.

"Dios mío, what the hell's wrong with me?"

Shame burns my cheeks as I draw the curtains, gathering my dress from the floor and quickly buttoning it. Backing away, I disappear into my bedroom and pull my suitcase from the back of my closet, my mind a cyclone of self-loathing and sadness.

My family is right. I'm just a pawn.

A stupid mouse who took the bait.

CHAPTER
Sixteen

SAM

It takes me less than sixty seconds to hack into her apartment's maintenance system and cut the lights dead. It takes me another five to pistol-whip her bodyguard so hard he'll be seeing double for a week. He doesn't look like the kind of fucker who'd waiver a shot at revenge, but I'll deal with that fall out later.

Lust and jealousy are dangerous weapons, and after watching Lola Carrera come so hard against a window the fucking glass fogged up, there's no army in the world that could stop me from sinking my cock into her pussy tonight.

"I'm leaving, Sam."

Never.

Her whispered admission sliced through the last strands of my sense and reason. Her breathless taunts made a bonfire out of my self-control. Lola is only going one way tonight, and that's with me. Predators don't barter with their prey. There are no pretty deals, sneaky underhands, or backstreet bargains. They stalk and they pounce, they steal and they break.

Her front door is open, and it smells like an invitation.

I don't make a sound as I slip inside, the heavy stillness crushing me like a velvet fist. I move slowly, cat-like, along the hallway, even though I know every inch of this apartment by heart. I head straight for the bedroom because that's where she's leading me. The sweet scent of her arousal is unmistakable beneath the generic florals and citrus.

I pause in the doorway, my anticipation turning my cock to stone. We're breaking the rules again. We're crashing through more unseen barriers. *Do bad things with me, Lola... Sharing our pleasure will be double the fun.*

I push the door open, the smallest creak shattering the silence. I hear her breathing in the darkness. *Rapid, shallow rasps.* Sounds that are so easy to make screams out of.

The curtains are closed. The moon is in hiding. I'm a thief in the night as I cross the room to reach the bed, stealing hearts and virtue with a fucking smile on my face. That's when she makes her move, darting for the hallway in a flurry of frantic footsteps. Her soft cry shatters the silence again as she runs straight into me.

I grab her arm and throw her up against a nearby wall, pressing a hand over her delicate mouth as my hips hold her body prisoner. "Strike a pose, *Lola Carrera*," I say huskily, drunk off her fury and her fragility. "The show's not over until I say it is."

Her muffled cries grow louder against my palm, and her sharp teeth snag on my skin.

Frustrated, I spin her around and crush my throbbing erection into her ass. *Holy fuck.* The feeling of her heat pressed up against me again is blowing all my late-night fantasies out of the water. It's enough to make my hand slip from her mouth.

"Get the hell off me!" She leverages her foot against the wall to try and tip me backward.

"Is that really what you want?"

"*Want?*" She toys with the word like it's an unwanted gift. "You don't *want* me, Sam Colton... Sanders... Whatever the hell your name is. You can drop the façade right now. I know where your allegiance lies. You saw Troy Davis roofie me, so you took your opportunity. You branded me for *him*... You branded me for *Dante Santiago*."

"I branded you for *me*." I drop my mouth to her shoulder as she hisses out a single rebuke.

"What about the other night? In the alleyway?" I catch the hitch in her breath.

"Don't deny you wanted it."

"Bullshit I did! It was sick. You're sick!"

"Then we'll be sick together." Incensed, I suck on her skin as hard as I can, creating another mark that won't be so easy to cover up. She yelps and shudders, but, again, she's not so easily conquered.

"My brother will be back any minute, and when he sees you—"

"He'll what?" I wrench her dress up around her hips, grinning to myself when she doesn't yank it back down again. "Tell me something, Lola... Is he coming here to drag you back to Mexico? Will you be a willing passenger, or will you be screaming inside the whole time because Daddy is taking all your dreams and wishes and drowning them in a river named Carrera?"

Her body sags. I've just deconstructed her truth into something real and ugly.

Like a bastard, I take advantage of the situation and ram my knee between her legs, spreading them wider.

"How long have you known?" she rasps. She's almost compliant as I brush my thumbs against the underside of her breasts.

"The day you started at Rutgers." I slide a hand between her thighs, trailing upwards; smirking as she pushes back on me, biting out a moan.

"That was over a month ago… Santiago could have come for me anytime—"

"But he didn't." I reach the damp apex of her thighs and slide a finger inside her panties. I'm so close to losing my shit over this woman it's unreal. One more breathy moan and I'll be destroying her virginity for the rest of the night.

"Am I supposed to offer my *gratitude*?" Hissing out the word, she tries to push me away again. "Do you know what he did to my mother eighteen years ago? *To me*?"

"Toss a story in the air and the facts will fall differently every time, Lola. Your father sent him and my stepfather an invitation to their own fucking murders. They got lucky. Your dad got pissed. Cue two decades of East Coast anarchy."

"You're a liar!"

"And you're a fucking lunatic," I snarl, losing my temper. "Flashing your pussy in that nightclub… Sucking that asshole's face earlier."

She stills. "Did you hurt him?"

"Damn right I did." I pinch her swollen clit in delicious punishment, inhaling her pained groans like they're oxygen.

"*¡Ay Dios mío!*" she gasps, and shudders, cursing me in Spanish. "*¡Hijo de su puta madre!*"

She's right. I am a son of a bitch. In more ways than one. At this, I drive my middle finger so deep inside her she loses her balance, slamming her palms against the wall as I circle and stretch her, prepping her for an even bigger surprise.

"You're crazy!" she cries, angling her hips for more.

"Crazy for you. Do you like it, Lola? Does it pique your interest? Are you going to climb down from your ivory tower to take a closer look? Maybe we should climb back *up* together?" With this, I give her exactly what she needs, ramming a second finger inside her. I pump mercilessly in and out of her body as she curses again.

"God, I hate you!"

"Feeling's mutual."

"You're a creep," she groans, squeezing my fingers as her pussy starts quivering.

"You're a tease."

"You're a filthy Santiago *pendejo*!"

"And you're *mine*!"

Ripping my fingers away, I spin her back around, smashing our mouths together to drown out her next insult. I taste peaches and cream, relief and desperation, before shouts and heavy footsteps in the parking lot outside send us spiraling back to earth.

Shit.

Tearing my mouth from hers, I slam my hand down in its place. "Don't make a fucking sound. I mean it, Lola. There's a fine line between the two factions of this war, and we're slow-dancing on the edge of it."

I think fast. I have exactly sixty seconds before Santi Carrera sees what I did to his second-in-command and starts redecorating her apartment in my blood.

There's a stairwell at the end of her hallway. It leads to the side of the building where my car is parked. I hear Lola's silent question in my head, and my mind is made up.

Wherever I'm going, she's coming too.

CHAPTER
Seventeen

SAM

I f looks could kill, Lola would have sent me to hell and back a couple of times over by now.

She's in the passenger's seat of my Bugatti, her hands tied to the Jesus handle above her head. I can't tell if she's madder at me for kidnapping her or at herself for coming all over my fingers as her brother was storming the stairs. We made it out with seconds to spare, and now we're speeding down the freeway and into the eye of the storm.

Not knowing Santiago's intentions toward Lola pushed my obsession into a wasteland of uncertainty. *And then she hit me with that sexy-as-fuck floor show.*

In that moment, ambition, lust, *Santiago*…all that other stuff ceased to exist. There's only her to drown in now, and what a great death it promises to be.

We drive for five hours straight, kissing the coastline all

the way up to New England. At two a.m., I see a derelict road sign for some roach motel a couple of miles shy of Newport, Rhode Island.

Pulling into the parking lot, I kill the engine.

"Are you going to play nice, Lola?" Turning to her, I trail a finger down one flawless cheek, feeling a surge of hope when she doesn't unleash a string of Spanish insults at me.

"You have no idea what you've done," she whispers, looking vulnerable and so fucking beautiful, I want to kiss all her doubt and hesitation away.

She's wrong. I know exactly what I've done. By taking her, I haven't just declared a new war on the Carreras, I've declared war on my own side too. We're on the run from the two biggest criminal organizations in the world, and I couldn't be happier about it.

I think I need a drink to process it, though.

"Let me go," she urges, her blue eyes wide and wary. "I'll tell Santi it was a mistake—"

"Didn't we cover this already?" Leaning over, I press my mouth against hers. *Will she bite me or accept me?* "There are no rules when it comes to you and me anymore, Lola. Only the ones we make together."

She rears back, her dark eyebrows drawing together. "Is it me you really want, Sam? Or is it my submission? When the sun comes up, will my heart just be another casualty of this war?"

I know what she's doing. She wants me to hurt her with a lie. She needs to convince herself that she's not a traitor to the family she loves. That way, she can absolve herself of the guilt she tastes when we kiss.

But absolution is for those without sin, and Lola Carrera and I have bathed in those bloody waters all our lives.

Sinking a hand into her hair, I twist the thick strands around my fingers and hold her so close we're sharing the same breath. "If all I wanted from you was a fucking conquest, *dulzura*, I would've spread your legs that night in my bedroom."

"But—"

"I want *everything*," I growl against her lips. "Every piece of you... Even the confused and broken ones you try to hide."

Those wicked blue eyes flash. "Then kiss me again," she says breathlessly, "and maybe I'll consider it."

Grabbing the back of her head, I crash our mouths together, swallowing every moan like it's a Michelin star meal. When she strains to reach more of me, I feel like I've won the moon and stars on a game of chance.

"How can you be so sure about us?" She breaks away again, panting.

"Because I *know you*, Lola Carrera." I hold her face prisoner between my hands, forcing her to look at me. "I know the pain you feel from this conflict. I know how much you hate smoking cigarettes, even when you pretend otherwise. I know your tiger spirit would have happily carved up Troy Davis's knee yourself if I hadn't beaten you to it... I love that when you look to the horizon it's the world you see, and not the borders of Mexico." I go to kiss her again. I can't help myself. "Stay awhile, little mouse. You might find you don't hate me as much as you think you do."

"That's a lot of hate to make right."

"Give me this night, Lola. I'll wrap it around us so fucking tight, you'll never want to break free."

"I'll give you more than that," she says, curling her arms around my neck as soon as I loosen her restraints. "But only if you swear it in blood."

The motel room is sparse, but functional. The whole interior is bathed in grays and browns, but her colors are blinding.

Kicking the door shut, I grab her by the wrist and spin her back into my arms for another violent kiss.

After that, clothes become skin, and heated promises take center stage.

Throwing her backward onto the bed, I pull her legs apart, impatient to taste every part of her. This time, there are no guns. No violence. Her body is a roadmap to her universe, and her hair is a messy dark web across the white pillowcase.

She tastes of *everything*.

"If this is what dawn feels like, I never want the day to end." With a groan, I drag myself away from her pussy, my chin glistening with the residue of her third orgasm as I settle between her legs. Holding her heavy-lidded gaze, I line my dick up for the ultimate prize. "Mine."

"Yours," she rasps, sinking her head back into the pillow, her small hands resting on my shoulders to brace herself.

With that one word, I drive in so deep her nails leave crimson welts across my skin, her slick warmth gripping me so tight I'm close to shooting my load right away.

"Harder," she whispers as I shudder to a stop. "Faster."

"Not if you want twenty-eight chapters and an epilogue," I gasp out.

She laughs softly and pulls my mouth down to hers. "I didn't know you made jokes."

"Not recently. With you, I'm relearning."

At that, she smiles.

"How much do you hate me now?" I say a couple of minutes later.

"Make me come again, and I'll tell you." Lifting her hips, she makes herself so full of me I can't tell where she ends and I begin.

We come together, and it's off-the-wall spectacular—a fucking fusion of lust, obsession, and everything that's perfectly imperfect about us.

Her back arches.

My mind is drunk.

Turns out, she doesn't hate me that much, after all.

She hates me even less when, lying tangled up in sheets and exhaustion, I give her my knife and instruct her to carve an L into my chest.

My oath in blood, just like I promised.

Two letters.

Two lives.

Two hearts that refuse to beat for a war that tries so hard to define them.

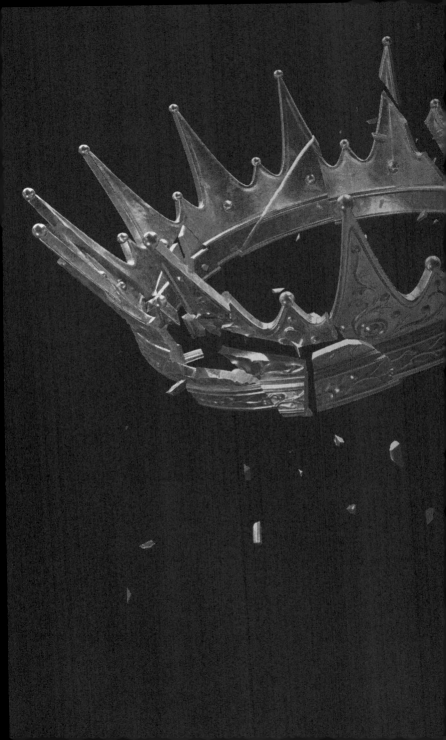

CHAPTER
Eighteen

LOLA

While my beautiful captor slept, I dressed in darkness and spilled our truth onto a dirty piece of motel stationary.

Now, standing by the bed and clutching the note in my hand, I'm as stained as the white sheet covering Sam's newly-branded chest. Unshed tears burn the back of my eyes as I reach down and trace a feather-light touch across the dark red L bleeding through the cheap linen.

"Mine," I whisper, echoing his earlier claim.

He doesn't respond. Those intense eyes remain closed as I trail my hand from his chest to his face. He's too lost in the depths of a dream to know what's about to happen. To understand why I have to go through with what I'm about to do.

It's not in spite of him. It's *for* him.

He asked me to give him the night, and I did. I gave him that and more. I gave him me—body and soul.

Heart.

And whether or not he believes it when he wakes, I've already given him all of my tomorrows. Every single one. But defiance always comes with a price, and ours is one I must pay alone.

For me.

For him.

For peace.

And for a chance at happiness for either of us.

I wish I could tell him goodbye, but I know he'd just try to stop me. He'd argue we could simply keep driving. Away from New Jersey. Away from Mexico. Away from the loyalties and responsibilities tying us to both.

But it would never be far enough.

Deep down, we both know it's impossible to outrun Valentin Carrera or Dante Santiago. Eventually, we'd be found, and depending on who got there first, one of us would answer with our life.

That's no way to live.

However, I'm leaving here more confident than I arrived. Thanks to Sam, I'm no longer afraid of who I am. By weakening me, he strengthened me.

Because of him, I found my voice.

Besides, if I've learned anything while being in America, it's that when something blocks your path, you don't try to run through it...

You find a way around it.

Fighting back the emotion threatening to bubble to the surface, I glance down at the paper in my hand, silently reading the words one last time.

The ones I stole from him and twisted into a fate I must endure alone.

When the mouse strays, she gets punished. Slowly and painfully until she wins her freedom. When that time comes, the hunt is on. Catch me, and I'm yours forever.

With a soft kiss goodbye, I place the tear-stained note on the nightstand and close the door behind me, returning to the chains he shattered.

———————

"What the hell do you mean you don't know where he is?"

I force myself not to flinch under the lead weight of my father's murderous stare. He's pacing the entire length of my apartment with Santi balancing out the act by marching his heavy-footed gait in the opposite direction.

They look like two pinballs bouncing off an electric fence. *If pinballs could raze an entire city with one glance.*

Valentin Carrera is one of the two most feared men in the world. Looking him in the eye with a lie on my lips is terrifying. My father loves me, but he also has the power to lock me away from civilization.

And from Sam.

"Just what I said," I say calmly while twisting my fingers into a pretzel. "I don't know where Sam went after I escaped, *papá*. He could be anywhere in the world by now."

Hopefully, I'm right, and he stays there until this storm blows over.

At that, my brother pauses, his gaze narrowing as he turns those accusing eyes my way. "And he just let you escape? Just like that?"

"Yep," I say, popping the "p" at the end.

"You want us to believe that Sam *fucking* Sanders went through all the trouble to carve up your skin, then kidnap you, only to decide you weren't worth the gas to chase down?"

I glare back at him. "You make it sound like he had a choice."

He lifts a dark, slanted eyebrow. "Didn't he?"

"No! I'm not some idiot college girl who can't fight her way out of a paper bag, Santi! I keep trying to tell you that" Folding my arms across my chest, I sink deeper into the leather cushions of my couch, adding under my breath, "You just refuse to listen."

"*Cielito*, you have to understand, you are priceless to us. If anything had happened to you..." My father's voice trails off, unable to simultaneously give voice to his fear *and* keep his rage in check.

The deep love in his eyes wars with the budding one locked away in my heart. The one I can never speak of for risk losing it forever.

I hate lying to them. The two men shoving their hands through their dark hair, carelessly dislodging both their favored slicked back styles while wearing out my hardwood floor, have always been my heroes. *My dark knights.*

But now there's another.

And his safety trumps my loyalty.

"I know, *papá*," I say softly. "And I'm sorry for the trouble I've caused Santi, and I'm sorry for worrying you so much that you had to fly here, and—"

"You didn't do anything, *cielito*. Once again, the

Santiagos have dared to tread on sacred ground. No man hurts my daughter and lives."

And that is exactly why I told them the story I did. Why, after skipping town, *hell, the state*, with Sam, and then showing back up nearly eighteen hours later to a *sicario* and testosterone infused apartment, I knew I had to do some fancy tap dancing to cover both our asses.

So, I lied.

I couldn't hide what we'd done. Not only did we leave a trail of destruction in our wake, but a neighbor saw us leave, giving the police a description of Sam's Bugatti and his license plate. By the time we made it to Rhode Island, the sharp jaws of truth were already snapping at our necks.

So I drew first blood.

I told my father and brother the story they wanted to hear. The story of how after Sam kidnapped me, I'd waited until he stopped for gas near New Haven, Connecticut, and then I'd run for my life.

The reality of what happened was substantially less dramatic.

The part where I hitchhiked my way across three states is true, however, I'd waited to call Santi until I was safely tucked inside the borders of New Jersey to give Sam plenty of lead time, not because I didn't have access to a phone.

I spoke nothing of Newport or the run-down motel where Sam's cock left a delicious scar inside me, matching the one carved on my skin.

When I finished, war raged across my father's weathered face.

A bloodthirsty look settled in my brother's eyes.

And me? I kept my silent promise to my darkest and dirtiest knight.

I did what I had to do.

I played the role of the virginal victim while painting him all the colors of a diabolical villain. If I knew it would've protected him, I would've happily shouldered all the blame. But my father and brother are so deeply entrenched in this Carrera/Santiago war, they wouldn't have believed me anyway.

A familiar lie is always more palatable than an uncomfortable truth.

That doesn't mean I don't have my own penance to pay.

My time in America is over. I'd already been ordered back to Mexico before Sam and I took off… After my return, I knew I'd never see the bright lights of the New York skyline again.

"Please, *papá*," I beg, fighting to knit the fragile fibers of peace back together as they unravel before my eyes. "Don't fan the flames of a war Santi and I will have to extinguish."

"Speak for yourself," my brother says, violence flickering in his dark glare. "I've been ready to fight this battle for years. All I needed was an excuse." One corner of his mouth tips up in a wicked smile. "So, I suppose I owe Sanders a thank you before I put a bullet between his eyes."

He might as well have fired it into my own chest.

"*Papá!*" I beg, turning toward the formidable man now looming over me. "Do something!"

"I am." Glancing toward the front door, he nods to where an expressionless RJ stands guard. "Tell the pilot to get the jet ready. My daughter will be arriving at Teterboro in half an hour." He snaps his challenge-filled gaze my way. "She's going home."

"*Sí.*" It's the first and last word RJ utters before pressing a button on his phone, a silent warning in his eyes. *Remember our deal...*

Three against one aren't good odds for anyone. But when you're the king's daughter returning from battle wearing the insignia of his sworn enemy, they're damn near impossible.

Closing my eyes, I soak in one final moment of freedom before wordlessly making my way toward my bedroom to pack up my new life...

And reluctantly return to the one I left behind.

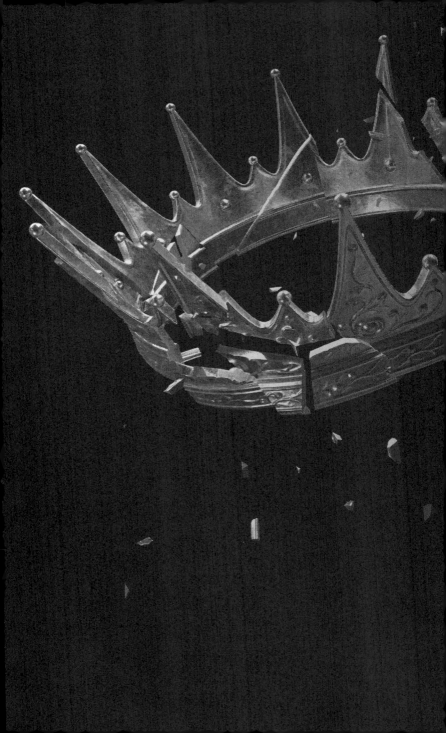

EPILOGUE

LOLA
Seven Months Later

"Hey, Daniela! Wait up!"

Adjusting the heavy backpack slipping down my arm, I smile at the bubbly blonde waving at me from across the quad. *Vanessa, I think is her name.* She's a nice girl, a little too talkative at times, but harmless.

I should know. My father and brother personally vetted every student on Northgate's campus. This place is nothing like Rutgers. With only two thousand students, it's almost impossible to blend in, so my family keeps their finger on its pulse, allowing no margin for error.

No dark corners for Santiago masks to hide.

Or so they think.

"Everything okay?" I ask, forcing as much of my native accent from the words as possible. No need to raise suspicion and make pretty blonde girls dead.

I laugh to myself. *Who knew that phrase could be used*

twice in one lifetime?

She nods, her pale cheeks stained red from the biting wind. "A few of us are going out tonight. You should come. We can celebrate your birthday."

"I'm not allowed to go to bars."

"This is college, not high school!" She laughs. "You're free to have fun, Daniela. Our parents have no control over us here."

Maybe for her. Her white-picket-fenced suburban life doesn't know a damn thing about control. About the dangers of bearing a name the world condemns as evil.

I grit my teeth as a looming shadow darts behind a lecture hall building.

Free is a four-letter word where I come from, nothing more. Especially now that I have twice the security. Luckily, RJ is family, otherwise Santi would've wasted no time in slitting his throat for failing to protect me from what he perceived as Dante Santiago's wrath.

Now *Miguel the Destroyer* has become my three-hundred-pound shadow, stepping where I step, breathing where I breathe. At any given time, he and at least three other men hover about, boxing me inside an invisible shield. One wrong move or misguided touch and the snow blanketing this campus will run red.

I shrug. "Maybe some other time."

There won't be a next time, and she knows it. Thankfully, she doesn't voice the questions pooling in her bright green eyes. "You're a mysterious girl, Daniela Torres," she mutters, walking away.

Daniela Torres.

It's the name my father assigned me before allowing me to return to the States with my entourage in tow. It took twenty-four long weeks of solitude and repentance to earn my way back into his favor. Mercifully, after six months of atoning for my sins in Mexico, *mamá* became my champion—the calm voice of reason in a chaotic war.

"Give her a second chance," she crooned into *papá's* ear. *"She's a free spirit, Val. A hummingbird thrives on perpetual motion. Clip its wings, and it dies."*

Mamá always had a way of bending *papá's* iron-will.

Begrudgingly, he conceded, enrolling Daniela Torres at a Newport, Rhode Island school where the biggest danger came from crossing the street.

I allow a secret smile to tug at my lips. I care nothing about this school. However, its location calls to my soul.

Because it's ours.

Making my way back to my heavily guarded apartment, I slip my key in the door as four shadows close in behind me. *"Buenas noches,"* I say in a sing-songy voice, bidding Miguel and his men goodnight with a private smirk.

Once I close the door, the air inside the darkened room changes. Turning the lock, I let my backpack slide off my arm while slowly drowning in the charged electricity of his presence.

"Did you miss me?" I whisper.

My answer is a firm grip around the back of my neck as I'm slammed against the wall, my pulse thumping a furious beat under his rough fingers. Sam doesn't greet me with a kiss or a soft caress. His greedy hands tear at my leggings until they're nothing but ribbons of confetti littering the floor.

"Catch me, and I'm yours forever," he growls, reciting the words from my note through clenched teeth. "Well, I've caught you, *dulzura*. There's no escape from me now."

The heat of his warning skates down my neck.

"What if I run?" I ask, biting my lip.

"I'll catch you again."

"What if I scream?"

His hand slides up my throat, gripping my chin and twisting it until it brushes his unshaven cheek. "I'll steal it from your lips."

"And if I fight?"

"I'll come twice as hard."

He seals his promise with a graze of his teeth against my jaw while thrusting a finger deep inside me. I moan at his rough possession. *This is the game we play.* Intruder and victim. The same act that started our torrid affair now feeds our addiction.

The dark can't mask what has only grown stronger with time. I feel him everywhere: in the air, on my skin, in my soul...

I spin around, and like two magnets, our mouths crash together, drinking the life from each other to soothe the thirst our separation caused. His bare chest rubs against my breasts, the scarred L carved into his flesh fanning the flames of my desire.

L for Lola.

L for lust.

L for love.

"Happy birthday, Lola." He hums out a dark, satisfied groan as his tongue laps my arousal off his fingers. He lowers his hand, and I shake in anticipation at the sound of his jeans unzipping. "What's your wish?"

"Freedom," I whisper, gasping as he pins my back against the wall. "Blood and salvation."

As I voice my demands, Sam grabs the back of my thighs and lifts me off the ground. Instinctively, I wrap my legs around his waist, crying out as he thrusts inside me, the searing pain easing the ache in my heart.

"Blood I can give you, *dulzura*. You have to earn the rest for yourself."

He's right. It's a battle fought with patience, not force. I'll embrace my role as a pawn in this cartel chess game. I'll move strategically across the board, hiding in plain sight from both deadly kings.

For now, we're forced to play by their rules.

But one day, I'll graduate. One day, I'll return to him, and we'll break these chains binding him to Colombia and me to Mexico. One day, we'll cross this thorn-riddled line drawn between our two families.

"For now..." I groan, his possessive thrusts driving me toward the edge of ecstasy.

For now, we'll meet in darkness.

Fuck in secret.

Love in silence.

Sam pauses, our bodies joined and aching for release. "And then what?"

I smile, soaking in the strained moments of peace before he shatters me once again.

"Checkmate."

ACKNOWLEDGMENTS

Cora's Acknowledgments

Catherine: Third cowrite down, forty-seven to go... Just kidding, kind of. Thank you for still wanting to write with me after the ridiculousness that was 2020. We made it. Here's to many, many more.

Ronda: Thank you for constantly reminding me who I am and what I'm capable of creating.

Crystal: As usual, thank you for always being there as a sounding board and remembering the details my creative brain glosses over. You're the best.

Gillian Leonard: I have no idea how you managed to edit and turn two back-to-back books around so quickly, but I love you to the moon and back for it. #teamkumquat.

KC Fernandez and Ronda Lloyd: Thank you for the fresh eyes and detailed proofread.

Ginger Snaps: You are my translation angel. Thank you for making sure I'm always authentic.

Carrera's Guerreras: You are one hell of a beta team. I don't tell you enough how amazing you are, so I'm doing it now. Love you all!

Cora's Twisted Alpha Addicts and Cora's Twisted Capos: Thank you for all your support and dedication to my work. I would be lost without you.

Danielle Sanchez and the staff of Wildfire Marketing: Thank you for always making me shine.

Lastly, to the bloggers and readers who enjoy and share my work, THANK YOU! Your support means the world to me. As always, without you, I'm just a chick with a laptop.

Catherine's Acknowledgments

To my husband and my two beautiful girls. I'm running out of adjectives again… Let's just say that I love how you bring me cups of tea and hugs when I'm writing. I love that I've inspired you to write yourselves. I just…love you.

Cora, my author guru. I would be hopelessly lost and clueless without you. Somehow, we did it. Not sure how... Thank you from the bottom of my green tea.

Sammy, Kathi, Sally, and Julia. Thank you for cheering me on from the sidelines. You've been there from the beginning, and you're more priceless than gold.

To my wonderful PA, Siobhan. Thank you for hopping aboard the Santiago show and for keeping my life in order.

And to my amazing Street Team for promoting me every day! — Joy, Jayne, Joanne, Ashley, Piia, Chelle, Janie, Isidora, Sarah, Tracey, Sierra, Sandra and Laura…

To all the book bloggers and bookstagrammers who are still taking a chance on a sort-of rookie. Thank you. Thank you. Thank you.

To Maria at Steamy Designs. Thank you for taking on all our demands, not disowning us, and for weaving your magic.
And finally to the readers. You make every invasive scan, test and operation worth it. I'll be writing these stories for you until they pry my laptop away from my lifeless fingers. Thank you for making all my dreams come true.

xx
#fuckcancer

ABOUT
Cora Kenborn

Cora Kenborn is a *USA Today* Bestselling author who writes in multiple genres from dark and gritty romantic suspense to laugh-out-loud romantic comedy. Known for her sharp banter and shocking blindsides, Cora loves pushing her characters and readers out of their comfort zones before delivering a twisted happily ever after.

Cora believes there's nothing better than a feisty heroine who keeps her alpha on his toes, and she draws inspiration from the strong country women who raised her. However, since the domestic Southern Belle gene seems to have skipped a generation, she spends any free time convincing her family that microwaving Hot Pockets counts as cooking dinner.

Oh, and autocorrect thinks she's obsessed with ducks.

For more book updates and news visit:
https://www.corakenborn.com

ABOUT
Catherine Wiltcher

Catherine Wiltcher is an international bestselling author of twelve dark romance novels, including the Santiago Trilogy. A self-confessed alpha addict, she writes flawed characters who always fall hard and deep for one another.

She lives in the UK with her husband and two young daughters. If she ever found herself stranded on a desert island, she'd like a large pink gin to keep her company... Cillian Murphy wouldn't be a bad shout either.

For newsletter sign-ups and book updates, visit
www.catherinewiltcher.com/newsletter

ALSO BY
Cora Kenborn

CARRERA CARTEL TRILOGY
(Dark Mafia)

Carrera Cartel: The Collection (*w/bonus novel*)

Blurred Red Lines

Faded Gray Lines

Drawn Blue Lines

CORRUPT GODS DUET
(Dark Mafia - Spinoff of Carrera Cartel)

Born Sinner (prequel)

Bad Blood

Tainted Blood

LES CAVALIERS DE L'OMBRE DUET
(Dark Mafia)

Darkest Deeds

Scarlet Mark (by Lexi C. Foss)

MIAMI BRATVA DUET
(Dark Mafia - Spinoff of Les Cavaliers de l'ombre)

Illicit Acts

Wicked Ways

LORDS OF LYRE SERIES
(Rockstar Suspense)

Fame and Obsession

Fame and Secrets

Fame and Lies

STANDALONES
(Dark/Romantic Suspense)

Sixth Sin

Cast Stones

STANDALONES
(Contemporary/Sports)

Shallow

Playboy Pitcher

Adrenaline

STANDALONES
(Romcom)

Unsupervised

Swamp Happens: The Complete Collection

STANDALONES
(Paranormal Romance)

Cursed In Love

ALSO BY
Catherine Wittcher

Cast Stones
Lovers & Liars

Made in the USA
Middletown, DE
22 October 2023